AN ALTERNATIVE IRISH CHRISTMAS

AN ALTERNATIVE IRISH CHRISTMAS

TRAMP PRESS

First published 2025 by Tramp Press, Dublin
www.tramppress.com

A CIP record for this title is available from The British Library.

10 9 8 7 6 5 4 3 2 1

Trade Paperback ISBN 978-1-915290-18-2
eBook ISBN 978-1-915290-19-9

Tramp Press gratefully acknowledges the financial assistance of the Arts Council.

Thank you for supporting independent publishing.

Set in 12pt on 16pt Devangari by Marsha Swan
Printed by L&C Printing Group, Poland

Contents

CARELESS PEOPLE

Jessica Traynor

He had read her journal. *Irish Wildlife Diary, 2024.* He knew he shouldn't even have picked it up, let alone opened it. But he was alone in the apartment, a rarity to the extent that he felt restless, wanted to somehow impose himself on the space. He had stood on the balcony for a while in the mizzling rain, until the blank stare of the surrounding windows began to feel oppressive. He had played PS5 with the match on in the background, but neither had held his attention. How many times over the past thirteen years had he wished for a bit of peace, a chance to zone out? Saturdays were quieter now, with Andrea off at her hiking club and Zoe between gymnastics classes and afternoons at her friend Sally's. Technically, he was on call to come pick Zoe up, which partly but not completely explained the restlessness. He found himself in her bedroom, depressed by its personality crisis: the pink fairy wings and soft toys of her younger years being edged out by make-up and skincare products and the jewel-coloured hairdryer with all its incomprehensible attachments that had cost them the guts of €500. The wildlife diary had felt knowable, somehow, the only object in the room infused with both her child and adolescent selves. He'd leafed through the watercolour illustrations of badgers and foxgloves and puffins, charmed by her handwriting – precise to the point of primness, except for her habit of drifting beneath the ruled line as she reached the righthand edge of the page, something he had himself done as a child. But then he read what she had written.

Andrea had arrived home soaked and mud-spattered after the fog that clung to the slopes of Lugnaquilla transmuted into proper rain.

Two months ago, she'd closed up her photography studio – a three-year attempt to run her own business. She'd got a good deal on rent in the wake of Covid and had thought that family portraits could cover her more ambitious shoots, but as the world returned to normal, rents had too, and nobody seemed to want pictures with their kids anymore. The studio had worn a hole in their finances that had gradually developed its own gravity, sucking in the small luxuries they'd thought they'd be enjoying at this stage in their lives – the last two years' foreign holidays, the upgrade to a better second-hand car, and ultimately, the house-deposit fund they'd slowly accrued.

Since the closure, Andrea had been withdrawn, spending weekends walking the hills with her camera, but (as far as he knew) taking photos of nothing. It was the first time he had ever known her to fail at something, and he wasn't sure how to talk to her about it. He assumed that she was talking to her friends in the walking group about it in any case – and although this was certainly convenient in terms of shielding Zoe from their worries, he sometimes found himself imagining their home as a rapidly emptying space.

Instead of saying any of this to Andy, he did the sensible thing and made her a cup of tea, before heading out in the car to pick Zoe up. He tried not to overthink his daughter's silence on the way home. Later, after she retreated to her room to message her friends, he'd sat watching Andrea doomscroll. 'We need to start thinking about Christmas.'

'I knoooooow,' she dragged her hands down her face. 'I think I'm coming down with a cold.'

'Sally is getting that new iPhone.'

'We're not doing that. The cost – and it's so fucking joyless.'

'OK so something joyful. For a thirteen-year-old.'

'Jesus Christ. Do you remember thirteen?' She eyed him over the top of her phone. 'Actually I bet you had a lovely thirteen. You were good at sports. And you were a boy.'

'It's shit being a teenage boy too. Surprise hard-ons. In the middle of maths class.'

'I just remember that age as – a blank. A big sad, unending blank. Like time had stopped, just as you inhabited your worst form.'

Her statement had filled him with alarm. She'd talked, before, about disliking her teenage years, but he'd never thought deeply about it. When they met in their twenties she was so self-possessed, almost chronically incapable of doubt, driving most of their decisions with a certainty that made his life very easy. He had never really believed she could have once been different. And Zoe – Zoe seemed the same to him.

'What about a dog?'

Andrea stared at him. 'A dog?'

Dogs were complicated, he thought. And dogs were simple. They had demarcated so many seasons of his childhood – family dogs, cousins' dogs. As the youngest of four brothers, his memories were often tinged with the confusion of trying to keep up with the older boys. Childhood holidays at his grandparents' house in Mayo, the sheepdogs would circle the boys like sentries: aloof but always there. Clearest in his mind were times spent alone with Guinness, their terrier-mix mongrel who would trot alongside him wherever he went. And the occasional pang when the dog would run to one of his older brothers instead of him. Dogs were the constant shifting weather of his childhood.

In more recent times it had sometimes struck him as sad that they didn't have a dog. Picking up Zoe at the school gates where the other parents stood chatting, their cocker spaniels and retrievers flapping sunnily by their ankles. He hadn't articulated this thought, busy as they were, and Zoe – surprisingly, he now felt – had never gone through the *I want a puppy* phase.

Áine in work was mad into dogs. In the past he'd looked upon her passion with the air of condescension people with children reserve for those who call their pets things like *fur babies*. Áine had three dogs. The first was a Jack Russell she'd inherited from a dead neighbour, and it barked all day while she went to work, so she got another one to keep it company. This was a greyhound, and she had got it for the calming effect it was supposed to have on the rabid Jack Russell. The greyhound was covered in suspicious scars and was stone mad. The two of them shredded her living-room furnishings and shat all over her house. It wasn't the destruction that got to him; rather, the tone of compassion she used when speaking about the situation, as if she was presiding over a complicated internecine conflict in an international court, and hadn't just stupidly, he felt, introduced two traumatised animals to a tiny one-bedroom house off Cork Street. But then, all of a sudden, the discussion at the coffee machine was all about a brand-new labradoodle, blonde and lamb-like, and the other two dogs weren't mentioned.

'How are the other two taking to the new puppy? Is it not utter chaos?' he asked one day, as Áine and Marie flipped through photos on her phone.

The atmosphere shifted. Was Marie glaring at him? Áine allowed an expression of resignation to settle on her features, as if she had explained the issue a thousand times, or as if he had asked her something inappropriate.

'We have a slow and steady system of integration in place,' she said, 'based on the dogs' needs.'

'Cool, cool,' he said, wondering who the 'we' referred to.

He suspected that Áine didn't like him much, but then he didn't like her either. She would certainly be the person to ask about dogs, though – even if it was only for him to learn which rescue centres to avoid.

'We're thinking about getting Zoe a puppy,' he said to her as a group of them from the commercial and marketing teams walked along the canal, back to the office from the good coffee place. It was a cold, bright morning and the leaves on the ground were filmed with frost. A solitary moorhen was swimming alongside them, propelling itself through the gelid water with sharp forward thrusts of its neck.

Áine looked at him with alarm, 'For Christmas?'

'No! I mean, yes I know Christmas is coming, but I mean … for life of course, for companionship.' He was floundering. 'Andrea has more time on her hands now that the studio's closed. And she thought it might be a good idea for Zoe. Zoe's … going through a bad time.' Bringing up the girls was cowardly, he knew.

'Well dogs are not a form of therapy.'

He bridled. 'I know that Áine. Therapy is therapy.' He finished with a clipped, 'Haha,' but a silence pooled between them.

'I want to make sure', he said, 'that we make the best choice for both Zoe and the dog – I mean, we want to avoid all the faceless DoneDeal puppy farms, but we're aware of our own inexperience. I don't think we'd be the right choice for a rescue with complex needs. I thought to myself that you'd have great advice to give,' he grinned, 'for eejits like us just starting out.'

He was laying it on thick, but she appeared mollified. 'There are some ethical breeders of course – I did such careful research before we added Effie to the family.'

'Of course.'

'Here,' she said, and took out her phone and swiped through some sun-drenched images on a profile. 'They've an Insta profile – Meadow Farm Puppies. You'll have to join a waiting list, though. They breed one litter a year, and they purposefully avoid the Christmas market. There are so many careless people out there.'

'Thanks.' He followed the profile on his own phone.

'Are you still on this puppy jag?' Andrea asked him as he gave her a lift to the station.

'Oh yeah – I got some advice from Áine in work about ethical breeders.'

'Sounds expensive. I thought we'd decided we were aiming for joy and not cost?'

'Yeah, but a puppy's not like an iPhone. It's not a status symbol. No one looks at a dog and thinks, *These people are showing off their wealth*.'

'Don't they?'

'Other kids don't. And we won't tell her the cost.'

'Can you tell *me* the cost?' There was a dangerous edge to her voice now.

He paused. 'Between five and seven hundred.'

'But … we don't have that much to spare?'

'We do, we do. Look, I know things are tight. My bonus this year should cover it.'

She looked sceptical. 'For a dog we don't want?'

'I do. I want it.' He glanced at her. 'And Zoe will love it.'

She grimaced, but said nothing, a movement he recognised as her internalising an argument. This was good. It meant he hadn't lost.

At work he scrolled through the Meadow Farm Puppy page, then on to other suggested accounts. The aim was to move far enough from the ethical centre that he could find a puppy in time for Christmas, but not so far that they'd end up with an animal both overbred and traumatised. So many of the accounts were from the US, but then one caught his attention. The location seemed to be somewhere outside Athlone. The photos were sparse but nicely taken. The environs recognisably Irish. A woman in her early forties with long ash-blonde hair and two dogs. Her face was mostly hidden in the photos, the focus on the dogs, frolicking in evening sunlight or along tree-shaded country lanes – a King Charles Cavalier and a Poodle. The resulting puppies she bred, once a year, were Cavapoos – medium-sized, fleecy-looking dogs of a smaller size and calmer temperament (or so he read) than the other must-have designer breed for 2025, Groodles. Last year's litter of six puppies each had a dedicated post, with updates about where they had found their forever homes. There were some reels, too, which he watched at his desk with the sound off. The camera work was a little shaky, as the woman was holding the phone herself, while a wriggling puppy nuzzled into and eventually got tangled in her hair. The woman's face was kind, her eyes surrounded with the kind of delicate fine lines that suggest frequent smiling and healthy hours spent outdoors. The video ended in laughter and a blurry view of the ceiling of whatever room she was filming in. The most recent post said that new puppies had been born, and to watch this space for photos. He messaged straight away.

> Hi I see you have a new litter and am interested in getting a puppy for our family, can you confirm if any are available?

Later that evening Zoe was sitting beside him on the sofa messaging on her phone.

'Aw Zo, look at these,' he said, playing the video of the woman with the puppy on her shoulder.

She scrutinised the video, watching it play twice in succession. 'Millennial pause,' she said.

'What?'

'Millennial pause. It's what older people do when they start filming, because they're afraid the phone isn't recording. Even Lady Gaga does it.'

Jesus Christ, he thought. 'OK, but what about the puppies?'

'They're so cute,' she said, and then – 'I love dogs,' the statement delivered again to her phone where three little dots bounced at the bottom of her screen.

Andrea came in carrying a book and her glasses and glanced at the reel. She shot him a questioning look, and he shook his head to signal to her not to say anything.

'Surefire way to get ringworm,' she said, 'letting them crawl in your hair like that. It often starts on the scalp so people aren't aware they have it.'

'Ew,' said Zoe.

He noticed a message had come through on his phone.

Thank you for your enquiry about Puppies.
Laura here. Yes some available.

That's great. How much?

€1200

OK. That's a little more than I'd
hoped. Going rate on Dogs.ie
is 5-7?

Understood. But this is a special litter.
Not listed on Dogs.ie or any website.
No one lists near Christmas. Too many careless people want Puppy for Christmas then abandon.
This was an unplanned litter (oops!) a one-off. Cost is higher because we don't want careless buyers.

OK. Let me think about it

Just be aware we only have 3 left. 2f 1m.

A picture came through of three Cavapoo puppies curled up together on a sofa, their button eyes staring seriously at the camera. One was russet, and two were a colouring he had learned was called 'apricot' – buff, with gingery traces around their ears and noses.

OK I'll get back soon.

A few nights later, in the pub with Andrea, he worked up the courage to broach the subject. Zoe was at a friend's house but would be dropped home at 11.30, so they had had to work quickly – a quick cocktail to start, a bottle of wine over a bolted meal, then a single post-dinner drink in the pub. He could feel the effects of the drink pooling in his limbs – he was stilled, Zen-like.

'How *is* Zoe doing, though? Is Zoe doing OK? Is she OK though, Zoe, do you think?' he asked.

The narrowing around Andrea's eyes suggested he had not been as subtle as he thought. 'I mean, she's fine,' she said, 'considering.'

'Considering …?'

'Oh the age. And girls. Two of them have turned on Sally.' She sipped her wine and grimaced. 'Fucking hell this is rank.'

'What did Sally do?'

'Nothing. Maeve and Fia have just decided. I'm surprised at Fia to be honest, she's a nice kid. But Maeve always seems to be at the centre of these things. Poor Sally. It's why she's being bought that iPhone for Christmas. I think her parents are hoping it'll be some consolation.'

'And have they had a go at Zoe?'

'No. but she's upset by it all. She knows it's not fair.'

'Well what do we do about it?'

She stared at him, alarmed. 'Do? We don't do anything. Anything we do will just make it worse.'

'That doesn't sound like good parenting?'

'There's good parenting,' she swallowed the last of her horrible wine, 'and then there's parenting a teenage girl.'

'This is all so fucking alien,' he said.

'Nope, it's endemic,' and then, 'Why the sudden interest in all this?'

'Don't say that. Don't say sudden, that's not fair.'

'Sorry, I didn't mean it like that.'

'I just … I never had this when I was a kid.'

Her face softened a little then, surprising him. 'You had other things. I mean, you dad …'

He said nothing.

The next day, he watched Zoe eating her breakfast cereal, nudging miniature shredded wheat onto her spoon, then raising it a little before pausing to stare out the window at a magpie on the balcony railing. 'Hurry up, Zo. Don't be so fucking dozy,' he heard himself saying, then wondered where that voice came from. She looked a bit wounded, leaving a few minutes later without giving him the small sideways hug she had developed over the past year in order to make as little contact with his body as possible.

He sat in work with a bitterness in his chest that could be heartburn. The Cavapoo Instagram page had been updated with a post showing the image of the three remaining puppies. It had over 500 likes and he was distressed to see comment after comment saying, *How much?* He messaged Laura immediately.

Hi there, me again. Would like to
take one of the puppies please.

He could see she was online, but she made him wait until lunchtime for a response, by which time his unease had blossomed into a headache, a tidal flow behind his eyes.

Hi, you are just in time. We have 1 female
puppy left. Her name is Charlie.

An image came through of one of the apricot puppies. She was adorable, but there was something that struck him as slightly uncanny, just at that moment, about the flat blackness of her eyes. Odd to have such unknowable eyes in a comically furry face. Like a teddy bear granted sentience. He pushed the thought aside.

She's perfect, we'll take her.
What are next steps?

Payment in three instalments. €200 due
now, €800 one week before pickup by
Revolut to cover all vet bills for treatments

and vaccinations. €2oo balance payable
by Cash at pickup. She will be ready to
leave the mother just before Christmas
so timing is perfect.
We will send regular Updates and
Pictures so you can keep track of her.
We will send address in advance of pickup.
Any questions just ask.

Thanks Laura. We're very excited
to bring Charlie home.

She sent through her Revolut details and he paid the deposit straight away. He waited a moment, and then texted his eldest brother, Rob, the one he still talked to sometimes.

Whatever happened to Guinness?

Fuck me, have they gone woke?

No haha the dog

I'll still drink it even if it's woke tbh. Pints?

Remember our dog Guinness?

Yeah??

What happened to her

???

He didn't respond to the final text:

You know what happened to her.

When he tries to remember the dog, she's a busy blur in the corner of one eye. Her barrel body thumping warmly against his calf. If he turns his mind's eye directly on her, she's gone, vanishing across the grass into the shadows at the edge of the garden he's dreamed up in order to stage this memory. His memories are like that: small fragments of film reel. It always seems to be evening, the low sun bouncing off breeze block. Or maybe that's just the tint that age is giving them. Andrea can speak for hours about her childhood memories. She thinks it's odd that he has so few.

'Have you told her about the puppy?' Andrea asked on a dark November morning. It was pissing rain, so everyone was about to bundle into the car to be dropped to various locations, which would make him late. Zoe was taking ages in the bathroom and he could feel a pinching at the edges of his lungs, like he can't quite fill them.

'*No,* no! It's a surprise, isn't it? Isn't that what we'd agreed?'

Andrea shrugged in a way that soured his anxiety into anger. 'We did talk about this Andy. Don't shrug.'

She sighed. 'She's asking about clothes vouchers.'

'What did you tell her?'

'Nothing. I said we had something planned. Will you just talk to her later? Manage expectations. Since it was your idea.'

'That tone's not helpful, Andy.'

'Oh fuck off,' she said, and they sat in the car in furious silence.

In the office, Áine was looking at him funny. He kept catching her, her doleful gaze carrying some kind of a premonition of injury. Like a dog about to be kicked – but she wasn't a dog, she was a 45-year-old woman, so his mind's drive to sympathy kept being cancelled out, an electrical current interrupted.

The hot-desking they'd brought in since Covid was a scourge, and because he'd got in late, he couldn't hide himself in the corner where the commercial team usually congregated. He put his headphones on – the big headset for making calls – as a signal that he wanted to talk to no one, but the only desk available was right outside the kitchen. He watched Áine, from the corner of his eye, taking prim little steps over to the sink and filling up her water bottle at the filter. Something about the way she unscrewed the lid, the little flourishes she made with her fingers, so unnecessary and self-conscious. Who was the performance for? As if anyone was watching, or would want to watch, this sad old bitch do anything.

He snapped his attention back to his screen but five minutes later she was hovering by his left shoulder as he tried to manoeuvre a particularly tricky graph from a PDF into PowerPoint. He refused to turn around until he felt the atmosphere congeal.

'How's the puppy settling in?'

'What puppy?' This was obtuse, he knew.

'The puppy you got for Zoe. Or did you decide against it?'

'No. We're getting it in a few weeks.'

'For Christmas?' she yelped.

'Yep.' He turned back to his screen, but she inserted herself into his line of sight.

'It's so irresponsible,' she started saying, her pale face quivering, 'I thought I made it clear—'

'You thought you made it *clear?*'

'How dangerous it is to buy from these breeders. The cruelty in how they treat the dogs, no better than battery hens. Only the most thoughtless—'

'Áine,' he heard himself saying, and his voice was almost tender, until it swooped up into a hoarse shout. 'Would you ever mind your own fucking business? Would you ever shut the fuck up?'

On Christmas Eve he'd had to park the car in a multi-storey near the office to be ready for the drive to Westmeath, to pick up the puppy. With the meeting with HR planned for the first week in January, he couldn't skip out early like he'd planned to, to beat the Christmas rush. He couldn't tell Andrea why work had suddenly become so inflexible, or that his bonus was gone. She was frustrated with his whole plan, culminating in this ridiculous trip to collect the puppy on Christmas Eve. Her displeasure had manifested in an increasing distancing of herself from the situation, creating a blast zone around a disaster. So she could abrogate responsibility, he thought, while offering no help whatsoever.

Google Maps told him the drive was an hour and a half, so he would make it for 6.30. He'd been apologetic with Laura about disturbing their Christmas Eve so late, explaining that living in an apartment meant they had nowhere to hide the puppy, and she had been accommodating if a little monosyllabic, sending updates and pictures of Charlie, the latest in front of the blurry ice-blue lights of a very overdecorated Christmas tree. In the back of the car he had placed a crate for the dog, water, food and a pink collar that he hoped Zoe would appreciate. Andy had picked it up and looked at it dubiously the evening before.

'Think she'll like it?' he had asked.

'It's very girly ...'

'What does that mean?'

'She's not a little girl anymore.' She had said it gently, but the exchange had opened up a small barren space inside him.

'It's just a collar. We can throw it out and get a new one.'

But looking at it on the back car seat charged him with unease. He pulled out his phone and checked Google Maps again, toggling the mode to satellite view to look down at the house he's visiting – a sprawling bungalow with a neatly tended if unlovely green space around it. The picture had been taken on a sunny day, the grass neatly mown. He could make out a red hay barn and two smaller outbuildings. An SUV of some kind was parked in the drive. He thought he would find the view comforting, but something about the contrast between this frozen sunny view and the dark pressing in around him felt disjointed. He clicked the phone into its holder and pressed the button to start the navigation.

The northbound traffic on the M50 was intense, Christmas-light-decked HGVs veering aggressively across the lanes. A guy in a Merc tailgated him, blared his horn, then overtook him before swerving across three lanes to make the turn-off for Blanchardstown Shopping Centre. On the other side of the road, he passed a collision between three cars; the road beyond rows and rows of static cars radiating light and rage. As the river of tail lights ahead of him blurred, he imaged the universe as a giant dark circuitry studded with angry red. He was the substance in between. It was a bleak thought, but a calming one.

The turn-off came, and he manually unclenched his shoulders. It was a wet night, the street lamps on the smaller roads casting glamourous swashes across the tarmac until they petered out, and he was driving on a dark laneway between hedgerows. Eventually, he found himself on one of those stretches of country road that widens out into a loosely gathered row of houses with a few street lights – a small ersatz suburbia in the middle of miles of fields. Google Maps pinged: *You have arrived at your destination.* He fumbled open the glove box and took out the envelope with its slim wad of twenties. The adhesive was yellow and brittle and wouldn't stick. He shoved it inside his pocket.

The house was facing away from the road, surrounded by high hedges. The driveway gate was closed, so he parked the car on the grass verge outside and cut in through an open pedestrian gate. The driveway took him round the side of the house, but even before he could see the house's facade, he knew something was wrong. There was no car in the driveway. The grass on the lawn had grown wild, and brambles had started to snake their tendrils across the concrete path. As the facade came into view, he could see its boarded-up front door, and two dark caverns where the picture windows either side had been smashed.

'What the fuck,' he said aloud, the sound muffled by the soft rain falling on the driveway. He pulled out his phone and called Laura, but there was an out-of-service tone. He peered at the screen and saw that her WhatsApp profile picture had vanished. He was shivering now, from the cold and the panic, and he jabbed again at the little green phone symbol on his screen, only for the out-of-service tone to blare at him again. He opened Instagram and searched her profile – nothing. Revolut too – *contact not found.* She had vanished. Or she never existed. He stood staring at the house. It was 6.45.

Then, something came bounding across the grass, moving from behind the house towards a shed at the garden's far edge. Too stocky to be a fox, too fast for a badger. As he stared, a familiar movement triggered recognition – the way its tail moved. A dog? It struggled through the half-open shed door and sure enough, he heard a bark, followed by a short whine so soft it was more like a rippling of air than a real sound. He staggered through the wet tussocks of grass, twisting an ankle in an unseen dip, wading onwards till he found a trail, a desire line winding towards the shed. The light of the street lamp was very far away, and the wet was soaking through his trouser legs, plastering them to his shins. The shed was long and low, covered in crumbling render, with its one window boarded up. A glass panel in the door was smashed, the door itself listing to one side, pulled off its hinges at the base. Tufts of fur were caught on the splintering wood around knee height where an animal had pushed through. He jammed his shoulder into the gap and heaved the door open. A cobweb flapped against his face, sticking to his lips. Before his eyes could adjust to the darkness, the smell hit him – a stench both intimate and sickly, curling up inside his throat. He could just make out the shapes of what looked like large rabbit hutches, piled and tossed against the back wall, their chicken wire torn and twisted out of shape.

'Here girl,' he whispered into the darkness, but nothing stirred. The ground was soft underfoot.

He moved forward, fiddling with the torch on his phone. It was then he felt the shattering, like a molar on chicken bone. He shone the torch down and saw them, at his feet and all around him, hundreds and hundreds of small bones, nestled on a carpet of what must be fur and shit. His foot had obliterated a small mushrooming dome – a skull. At first, seeing their tiny heads nestled above the delicate rib cages, he thought they must be babies, but then he saw the corpses farther back, almost mummified, their pelts shrunk over protruding ribs and haunches. When he backed out of the shed, he felt the silence creeping back like an animal reclaiming its territory.

In the car on the way home he cancelled Andrea's call and pulled onto the verge. His throat was stinging from the bile that he had swallowed. He clawed at a tuft of fur on his jacket – black and white. Not the apricot he had been promised.

He typed a message to his brother:

What happened to Guinness?

He could see Rob was online. He watched the dots bounce and stop, bounce and stop.

Jesus man, Happy Christmas?? I thought you were being a dick bringing it up.
And then I thought that maybe you don't remember. You were only small.
She wasn't allowed in the house and you kept bringing her in. Every time one of us turned our back you'd be opening the back door for her.
And one night Da came home and we didn't realise you had her in. And you never saw the worst of him but he was bad that night – shouting and screaming.
And she went for him. The gentlest dog in the world and she went for his ankle.
Didn't break the skin or anything, but still.
He kicked her about a bit, but it must have been worse than we realised.

> He locked her in the shed. When I went in
> in the morning she was dead. Just
> slumped down on her side all stiff like
> she'd been hit by a car.
> I can't remember what we told you,
> but I always thought you knew. Sorry.

He dropped his phone on the front seat and reached back for the pink collar. It seemed so implausibly small and empty now, a little noose, a porthole on the dark. He ran through how things would go at home – the argument he and Andy would have once Zoe was in bed. The question over whether to compound it by telling her he had lost his bonus. And the Christmas morning with nothing to offer Zoe but a pink collar that a little girl who didn't exist might like for a dog that didn't exist either. And himself standing like some idiot stranger in the middle of their home, with nothing useful to offer. He knew that Andy would fix things, that before the argument even ended, she'd have put some clothes vouchers on their strained credit card. But as he pulled out into the long dark of the night, the images spooled out like a reel in his head: his daughter who wanted to die opening a box that couldn't be filled.

WE NEED TO TALK ABOUT CHRISTMAS

Sophie White

I fumble in the sheets and answer my phone before even looking at the name. Not checking is a mistake. It's her. Loins of my fruit. Does that work? You get what I mean. My mother.

'Ellie. Are you there?' She shouts as though phones are mere props and she, in fact, needs her voice to travel over great distances to reach me.

'Yes, Mum. I'm here,' I try to keep the sigh from my voice as I squint at the digits in the corner of my screen. It's after 7am, the morning light blazes in my bedroom. My bedroom that is also my living room that is also my kitchen, and so on.

'We need to talk about Christmas, Ellie.'

'It's August, Mum. And it's 7am.'

'It'll creep up on us before we know it.'

'Mmmmm,' I switch to my Bluetooth headphones so I can make better use of this time that I must listen to my mother rattle through the Christmas plans with the fervour of someone saying a decade of the Rosary. I move to the kitchenette and start to make coffee. I work fifty-five hours a week in digital-content creation so that I can afford to live on my own in Dublin. Sadly, all this affords me is a studio where I could quite feasibly prepare breakfast while sitting on the toilet. The convenience!

'I am happy to prep food here, if you host,' my mum is speaking in a rush, as though concerned I will be cutting her off at any moment, even though I have long abandoned trying to curtail the Christmas talk. Once she's going, she's unstoppable.

'I'll do my tomato soup to start.' It's her usual script.

My mother has a psychic connection to Christmas that borders on mania. If she had her way, we would commence talking about 'next Christmas' on the twenty-sixth of December. As it is, it has taken years for me to beat her back to a slightly more reasonable time to begin 'talks'.

'Soup is very filling.' I say as always. 'The meal is so big … do we need a starter?'

I pour water over my ground coffee and line up a frankly deranged number of supplements. I'm forty-two and have lately embarked on a new health kick that I call, *throw shit at the wall and see what sticks*. I read that loneliness is a bigger health threat than smoking, but rather than encouraging me to treat my loneliness with drop-in pottery classes and Hinge, and other things Millennials are clinging to, to beat back the despair, this statistic has only served to nudge me closer to taking up smoking. If the loneliness is already killing me, I may as well be sucking back some modicum of enjoyment.

'Oh Ellie, my tomato soup is Paul's favourite.'

It is apparently entirely irrelevant that Paul will not be at Christmas dinner. He wisely fled to Australia years ago, got married and swiftly produced three children, aka ironclad excuses to never come home.

'Will we see a bit closer to the time how we're feeling?' Futile plea on my part.

'We'll have the turkey of course. I'll do my spiced beef. You'll do the ham.'

I push the plunger on my pot of coffee and visualise pushing my irritation down also. In my head, I scroll forward to the meeting in Boardroom Four at 10am. 'Bennets Stores' Pitch Brainstorm' has squatted ominously in the middle of this week since July.

'Ellie? You'll do the ham, won't you Ellie?' Her tone has pitched upwards to panic.

'We don't need three meats, Mum. There's two of us. We could practically halve a chicken breast and be done. Especially with the soup.'

She ignores this entirely. Any dissent on the meat front is like an affront to her religion. 'I'm writing down "Ellie – Ham".'

I can even hear the scratching of her pen. I can see her sitting on the painfully upright and uncomfortable chair in her draughty little flat, phone urgently pressed to her ear.

'Mum. It's August. I'm not talking about Christmas until October.'

I end the call before I add anything hurtful.

'Right gang. Time to talk about Christmas.'

In Boardroom Four a couple of hours later, I am regretting the high-waisted trousers that felt aligned with my new resolution to appear like I care in work. In a more general way, I am regretting every macro-decision (nonsense degree in 'Multimedia') and micro-decision (*Sliding Doors* inspired pixie cut in 1999) over the last twenty years that has led me to this moment, sitting opposite Private School Tristan as he announces that we must talk about Christmas.

Having so recently escaped one Christmas conversation in August, it feels like a very particular injustice to be back on the topic, trapped in this long windowless room choking on the fug of other people's morning breath.

Of course, if I'd been feigning even the remotest bit of interest in my job in the last decade, I'd probably have taken on board by now that in August all eyes in every advertising and digital-content agency must turn to the now-yearly competition between department stores and brands to create the most tear-jerking, heart-wrenching, nostalgia-baiting Christmas advert possible. The greatest hits of the genre include the, now canon, John Lewis ad of 2015 'Man on the Moon' in which an elderly granddad is marooned on, you've guessed it, the Moon, and excluded from all Christmas festivities. That ad sparked a sort of Sad Ads arms race among department stores and supermarkets, with each doggedly pursuing the ultimate three-minute Christmas content that would unravel even the most emotionally numb and stunted among us.

A few years ago, Jeff Bezos gave us a machete straight to 'the feels' – as they say in my interminably annoying office –

about an older woman who'd been creepily tracking the young girl next door and concluded that she was anxious. In what is surely a bit of an overstep, the woman went on Amazon and had a bird feeder sent to her. The tagline was 'Kindness. The Greatest Gift.' The comments on the YouTube version were turned off. They wouldn't want anyone to point out the hypocrisy of preaching kindness while not exactly being known for showing kindness to their own employees.

I think the reason I am so bad at this part of my job is because all of the 'sad' Christmases look so appealing. A trip to the Moon to wait out the season of 'joy'? Yes please, 384,400 km is just enough distance between me and my mother. My mother is a bit like the Moon. She lacks the gravity to keep the people she loves with her. Me, my brother, my dad – though in my dad's case death is what's causing him to keep his distance, so not exactly my mother's fault.

A buzz of my phone on top of my notebook draws my eye. I can see a message from her. *I'll get the Christmas pudding started.*

Private School Tristan is looking at me now. He's said something to me. Banal, no doubt. When someone speaks in such meaningless generalities as Private School Tristan, it's always fine to answer with similar.

'Ohmigod! I know what you *mean*!' I return smoothly with a grating pep that matches his energy. 'The thing I love about doing this every year is how we get to really dig into the human condition and also showcase our clients' own humanity. Companies are always cast as these faceless, nefarious entities … but we're all just people, right?! People just *trying* … yanno?'

This inspires vigorous nods from my colleagues, Texts With Keyboard Sound On Deb and Thumb Ring Steve across the table. Of everyone, only Tuna Pasta Bake In The Microwave Marie looks wise to me. She purses her lips to hide what I can see is an appreciative smirk.

Tuna Pasta Bake In The Microwave Marie and I have something that could drift into friendship if either of us were that kind of person. As it is, she occasionally gives signs that she's on to me, and is not unsupportive of my ways. And I, in turn, don't hold her reheating of fish as much against her as I would somebody else.

'Beautifully put,' Thumb Ring Steve aims a finger gun at me, which I pretend to receive with bashful gratitude.

'So. Ideas.' Private School Tristan strides to the top of the room where a whiteboard hangs.

Texts With Keyboard Sound On Deb flips open her iPad cover. 'I'm going to jump in with something a little left field but what about …' – a pause for us all to prepare for this incredible innovation – '… humour?'

At this I feel the first flicker of enthusiasm I've felt all day.

As Private School Tristan writes 'Humour' on the board, I pounce to shit on Texts With Keyboard Sound On Deb's idea.

'Hasn't played well in the past.' I snap, clicking my pen on the dismount.

'How has humour not played well?' Thumb Ring Steve demands.

'The banned Mr Kipling ad. Aired 2003. Depicted a nativity play directed by Mr Kipling featuring Mary graphically giving birth. Tagline was "Has Mr Kipling ever directed a nativity play before? No, but he does make exceedingly good cakes."'

'That's genius!' Private School Tristan laughs.

'Eight hundred very vocal Christians didn't think so.' I shrug. I can pass whole meetings shitting on ideas. It's like a very satisfying cardio.

Texts With Keyboard Sound On Deb clears her throat, ready to keep pushing her groundbreaking idea to do an ad with humour. 'That was more than twenty years ago, Ellie. We've had more edgy stuff since then. Audiences have a much higher tolerance for these things now.'

I'm quick off the mark: 'In 2017, Greggs had to apologise for their Christmas ad wherein they cast a Greggs Sausage Roll in the part of Baby Jesus.'

Private School Tristan intervenes to cast the deciding vote. 'Amazing suggestion, Deb, but I think the client is really looking to go with the emotional angle. It's Christmas, it's one of the few opportunities of the year when big business can foster a bit of warmth from the general public. So "feelings-wise" what are we thinking?'

'Sad old people?' Tuna Pasta Bake In The Microwave Marie suggests.

'Unfortunately, old people aren't testing well anymore. Now that most of the sad-old-person cohort are Boomers, consumers are responding less favourably. It's the wealth hoarding, and such.' Private School Tristan shrugs.

'Sad children?' Thumb Ring Steve tries.

'Sad children are tricky to navigate.' I'm back in to naysay once more. 'You constantly run the risk of being accused of exploitation in service to an emotionally manipulative festive cash-grab.'

'What if there was a charity partner? We'd have our arses covered. A terminally ill child celebrating its last Christmas would be amazing.' Thumb Ring Steve claps his hands delighted.

'Interesting,' Private School Tristan nods slowly. 'Could we go sadder, but less grim?'

Purely to amuse myself I throw out an idea. 'What about a daughter who was abducted years ago and held captive in a basement returns on Christmas after twenty years missing? "The best Christmas presents can't be bought, but for everything else … there's Bennets Stores."'

'Adore.' Private School Tristan abbreviates this idea to 'Kidnap Christmas' on the board.

Ugh. That is the danger in throwing out the most ridiculous ideas for your own entertainment in advertising: often they're the very ones everyone latches onto. Suddenly you're being congratulated endlessly for your objectively ludicrous suggestion. My Durex campaign was one of my worst blunders. It showed parents Googling *how do I find out about sex offenders in my area*, with the tagline 'Skip the Hassle with Durex.' Thank God people with actual sense panned it on socials and got it removed.

'What about a dead pet?' Texts With Keyboard Sound On Deb is back, keen to redeem herself.

'Me likey,' says Private School Tristan in what has to be the most embarrassing phraseology of all time. 'Survey after survey's concluded that people care way more about animals than people. Would we do Sad Pet rather than Dead Pet?'

'I think I've got all our boxes ticked,' I lean forward. 'A sad old person dies at home at Christmas. Dog is starving but stoically refrains from feasting on his owner's remains. On Christmas Day, the neglectful kids of sad old person arrive to find the dog nudging a gift into the hands of the corpse.'

The silence that greets this baffling idea is immensely satisfying and I settle back in my chair happy that I won't need to contribute again today.

Then to my horror, Thumb Ring Steve takes up the batshit baton. 'So good! The tagline could be "Sometimes only your best friend knows what to get you."'

Goddammit.

Another text from my mother alerts me to the alarming fact that she's going to start dropping over Christmas decorations to my flat every couple of weeks for the next few months as there's too much for one carload. Since her move to the assisted living we do Christmas at my home, making it even more inescapable.

I pick up the phone to subtly type a text reminding her that I live in a 300-square-foot studio.

Undeterred, she replies promptly. *Sure most of the Christmas bits hang from the ceiling, Ellie.*

I shudder with a flashback of last year, endlessly dodging a garrotting by the expandable foil garlands, stars and giant bells that my mother favours. The level of ceiling coverage is oppressive in the already-too-small space, but I know she won't be dissuaded.

Another text informs me that I've been relieved of ham duties, but am to make the roast potatoes.

As the others continue to riff on other banal ideas, I rolodex through the catalogue I keep in my head of my mother's ailments. She's nearly eighty, but her decline has been frustratingly slow. She's got a bad hip. A bit of psoriasis. Nothing that's going to take her down between now and December. I think about all the posts I see on social media from people talking about rejecting their toxic parents and 'families of origin', about finding refuge in their 'found families'. I admire their grit, to be honest. It takes a lot to get out of a family. Though I imagine their resolve is informed by traumas far worse than those inflicted by my mother on Paul and me. You can't really emancipate yourself from your mother simply due to monumental levels of irritation. Even *I* can see that's a pretty hard line to take. I'll suffer another Christmas and see her on her birthday. Maybe by next Christmas the hip will have brought her down a flight of stairs.

Private School Tristan's tapping of a new phrase on the board catches my attention.

'Relatable but niche.' He underlines this.

'As we all know, the memes and clips that perform best on socials are ones that are, somewhat paradoxically, both relatable and yet niche. I've been wondering if this isn't an interesting avenue to explore for the Christmas ad. Who have we not seen represented in Sad Christmas Ads before now? Is there a way to blend "sad" with "niche" and "relatable"?' Every time he makes the air quotes, I have to consciously refrain from visibly cringing. He continues, 'And also – buzzword alert! – what about "community"? Maybe even with a bit of humour? Tonally it's a balancing act, I know, but this could *really* set us apart this year.'

Despite my resolve to sit out the rest of the meeting, an idea nudges me. The found-family people never feature in the ads. A series of scenarios line up like dominoes. Surely there are plenty of people like me who wish they could get out of their family Christmas. Don't *these* people deserve to have a happy Christmas too? To spend Christmas with people they actually like?

I relate these thoughts to the group who seem to warm to the new direction.

'How would the protagonist get out of their own family Christmas?' Thumb Ring Steve enquires.

'The only way I'd get out of Christmas dinner with my mother would be to fake my own death,' I say brightly. 'We could do that, and it would bring a bit of levity to the ad!'

I seem to have the support of Tuna Pasta Bake In The Microwave Marie who laughs appreciatively.

'We could do a montage of her previous bad Christmases with her family, so we don't lose audience sympathy.'

'I'm not sure faking a death is very festive for an ad.' Predictably, Texts With Keyboard Sound On Deb has no vision. Or actual knowledge of our industry.

'Not to contradict you there, but actually there's precedent for it. In 2015 the German chain Edeka featured a Sad Old Man faking his own death to lure his family to spend Christmas with him. My suggestion playfully turns this on its head. Then when our protagonist is "dead", they're free to celebrate with the people they truly feel at home with.'

'You're selling me, you're selling me.' Private School Tristan is nodding approvingly. 'It's genuinely innovative but also speaks to the very real and difficult circumstances of people who need to *make* their own families. It's beautiful Ellie. Let's formalise the pitch and submit it to the client for approval.'

FOUR MONTHS LATER

'Happy Christmas darling!!!' My mother is at the door along with a man I don't recognise who is holding a vast dish of trifle.

'This is Ben,' she bustles in, dragging the plaid shopping bag on wheels that she adopted when she turned seventy. 'He's my taxi man and Christmas dinner Sherpa!'

Ben hands me the trifle and winks at me. 'Happy Christmas.' He calls to my mother, 'I'll be back up with the meats now.' And heads away down the hall.

In the kitchenette, my mother is glaring into the oven. 'Ellie there are six roast potatoes on that tray!'

'There's two of us! And you've insisted on three types of meat, including a 12 lb turkey.'

'Well thank God, since there's apparently a potato famine in your oven.' She straightens up and scans the rest of the room. 'Barely a decoration up,' she sniffs.

Ben reappears with a crate bearing three tinfoiled lumps, each about the size of a toddler. I step forward to take it, but when I stagger slightly he helps me carry it to the counter.

'Thank you, Ben.' I say. 'Could I interest you in 10 lbs of turkey meat?'

'Haha. Enjoy ladies, I'll be off.'

'Thank you, dear!' my mother calls from her perch on the end of my bed where she's adding an expandable foil Santa to the explosion of other foil already dangling from the ceiling. I only debate giving her a firm push for fifteen seconds or so.

'Right. Soup is in the Tupperware in the shopping bag,' she clicks her fingers at me to retrieve it. 'I also made a loaf of brown bread.'

'Mum … It's all too much.'

'For God's sake, Ellie. You're hardly some delicate thing with a birdlike appetite. You're obviously putting away plenty of food the rest of the year.'

After soup, I hack at the beef, ham and turkey and load the plates, trying not to look at the trifle and Christmas pudding lying in wait over by the microwave.

My mother has always specialised in punitively enormous Christmas dinners. I'm convinced it's designed to immobilise whatever poor person is present and prevent them from fleeing her exhausting company.

'You've barely touched the bread sauce,' she glares at me across the tiny table, which is so overrun with all the Christmas trimmings, we've had to place said bread sauce on the floor beneath, along with the cranberry sauce, overflow gravy and tray of extra stuffing.

'I had bread with soup, I'm eating meat stuffed with bread, and now a sauce of bread. I literally can't, Mum.'

It's taking me so long to plough through this plate teeming with food that it's somehow already on the turn. The edge of the puddle of gravy has taken on the firmness of the jelly pet food is usually suspended in, while the surface of this faecal puddle is forming a puckered skin. On the counter behind my mother, the gaping carcass of the turkey regurgitating pork stuffing keeps catching my eye. Determinedly, I keep pushing down one forkful after another. I put a chunk of spiced beef in my mouth and will myself to chew and swallow. Inside me, the food piles up all the way to the back of my throat, so the last bite requires a strenuous swallow.

'I'm done, Mum.' My words are strangled.

'There's still trifle,' she smiles. 'And the pudding of course.'

'Yeah. But … will we take a gap for a bit? Digest.' I ease myself to standing, grateful for the forgiving leggings I have on under my dress.

'Alright,' she puts her cutlery together. 'Will we watch a bit of telly? *Mrs. Brown's Boys Christmas Special* is probably on soon.'

'Lovely.' Opening my mouth even just to speak feels risky in case the final bite of spiced beef triggers a revolt in my oesophagus.

She takes the one armchair – having never had anyone but her to visit, the purchase of a second feels unnecessary. I sit on the end of the bed wishing I could lie all the way down and not move till January. We sit in a sort of relieved silence as the Christmas TV schedule does that thing that every Christmas TV schedule must do: remove all need for familial interaction. There's a children's choir singing a selection of depressing religious carols. We watch a bit of *The Wizard of Oz* then switch over to RTÉ to await the start of *Mrs. Brown's Boys*.

That's when it happens.

An ad opens on a forlorn woman in her thirties, washing dishes and looking out at a snowy scene. A message plays aloud from her phone. 'Susan,' the voice is hectoring. 'It's your mother. We have to discuss Christmas. I know it's a while off, but it'll creep up on us before we know it.'

I glance nervously at my mother who is watching with interest. She looks over. 'Is this your agency? Exciting!'

On screen, as the mother continues ranting about trifle and Christmas pudding, a series of flashbacks play of the forlorn Susan's grim childhood Christmases complete with angry mother, cowering brother and silent father.

In the next scene, Susan is in the office being asked by a colleague about her Christmas plans. Susan gives a desolate-sounding, 'probably just the usual'.

Days on a calendar scroll forward with the mother's domineering voice announcing she'll be over first thing Christmas morning.

In the next scene, Susan talks to her brother: 'It's easy for you, you're in Australia. With Dad gone, I'm stuck alone with her.'

My mother's eyes whip to me at this and then back to the screen, which she leans closer to.

I wonder if I should've taken more pains to obscure some biographical details. Though I feel safe enough. She's a toxic narcissist and toxic narcissists never recognise themselves to be toxic narcissists; they're too self-absorbed.

The ad unfolds with Susan's fake death – a fatal winter hiking accident, a friend pretending to be from emergency services phoning the mum, explaining how no body has been recovered – I'll admit all this requires a fair bit of suspension of disbelief but we felt it worked. People will swallow a lot of shite at Christmastime.

I watch my mother's hunched shoulders stiffen as the final scene plays out. A cosy house, a gaggle of friends with crackers in party hats. The ad's tagline appears over the scene.

Christmas together doesn't have to mean misery.
Choose your own family this year.
And choose Bennets Stores.

My mother slowly sits back in her chair.

'I see, Eleanor.'

'Will we get the trifle?' I deflect, my confidence in my subtlety dipping slightly.

'You think Christmas with me is such a hardship?'

'What? What are you talking about Mother?'

'You clearly wrote that ad.'

'Don't be ridiculous, Mum. My agency made it, that's all.'

'The dead father, the brother in Australia. The pudding and the trifle.'

'Lots of people have dead fathers and family in Australia. And everyone in Ireland has pudding and trifle.'

'Well, I won't be having any.' My mother rises, carefully minding her hip. She moves toward her coat on its hook.

'Ah Mum, c'mon.'

She turns to me smiling and shaking her head. There's something off in her expression though and then I realise what it is. It's the most honest expression I've seen on her face in years. There's no veneer of pleasantness. No look of practised patience that I'm not sure I realised had been there all this time.

'Oh, Ellie. You don't even realise, do you? You're not stuck spending Christmas with *me*. I'm stuck spending Christmas with *you*.'

I stand to face her. 'What are you talking about?'

'Paul asks me. No, he *begs* me to come to them in Melbourne every single year. But if I went, who would spend Christmas with you?'

I don't have a reply for this. It feels too damning to say, *No one*.

'No, I'm stuck with you, I'm afraid. Who else would stay? Sure Paul left the house the second he could. And then the continent. And I'm not saying you took years off your father's life, but living in an atmosphere of such profound negativity isn't good for anyone. I only wish he'd made it till you'd moved out.'

I sit back down heavily.

'You're not the *girl* in the ad, Ellie. You haven't "chosen your own family" have you? Is there anyone who'd come to pull crackers with you? No, you're the self-centred, unpleasant person that everyone feels obliged to see at Christmas.'

My mother pulls her coat on, opens the door, then hesitates a moment before sweeping into the kitchen. She tucks the pudding into the crook of her elbow and takes the trifle.

'On second thought, I will be having these.'

ADESTE FIDELES

Mike McCormack

She did not look as if she was used to knocking on strange doors at any time of the day, much less so late in the year. My own anger on seeing her standing there couldn't have helped.

'No,' I barked, 'no more interviews, I've had enough.'

The way she stepped back and raised both hands in a bid for patience stopped me from slamming the door in her face.

'I'm not here for an interview,' she said, 'I'm here to say thanks.'

I stalled closing the door in mid-swing. She dropped her hands to step forward.

'I just wanted to say thanks, I'm one of those who—'

'I know who you are.' And that was all I could manage as we stood facing each other.

For some reason I believed she had come a long way. The stiff way she carried herself suggested she had put miles behind her. Though she looked tired, there was something other than fatigue that had put those lines through her face. Martha shouldered her way into the door beside me, the same angry impatience rolling off her in waves.

'No,' she said bluntly, 'no more fucking interviews, haven't you people had enough?'

I raised a hand. 'It's OK, Martha,' I said, 'it's not an interview.'

'A word of thanks,' the woman added. 'I thought it was the least I could do.'

It was late afternoon, light was failing. It would be dark in another half-hour and this pilgrim – that was her appearance in the shadowed light – would be carried away in the same darkness. Anger and impatience twisted against each other within me.

'You could have sent a card,' Martha said, 'it would have done the job just as good.'

The woman reached into her jacket and pulled out a long envelope. She handed it to me before I could think to refuse. 'I did write this, it's just a short note. And I thought about posting it but that seemed ...' It was curious to see her scramble for words when everything up to this suggested she was unusually dauntless and self-willed. 'I didn't think it was appropriate or proportionate to the task,' she continued. 'But I have delivered it now and I am not going to take up any more of your time. Goodbye and I wish you both, and Elern, a happy Christmas.'

She turned on her heel and walked away. Another two paces would take her beyond the porch light into the encroaching darkness.

Martha stepped in front of me. 'Wait,' she called, 'you can't go like that. Come in for a moment.'

The woman looked thinner and older in the light of the kitchen. The rain gear and strong boots that gave the suggestion of a long trek behind her was borne out in the cold roses of her cheeks. She pulled a chair from the table. I offered her tea.

'Tea would be nice, thank you.' She unwrapped her scarf and put it across her knees. 'I can't imagine that I'm the first one to come to your door with a word of thanks.'

'Yes,' Martha replied, 'You are the first. To tell the truth it has never crossed my mind that anyone should come and say thanks.'

Martha had taken a seat opposite her and was looking at her keenly.

This whole set-up was making me very anxious. This could go either way.

'I read about Elern and all the other donors.' She paused then as if sensing that her next utterance was delicate. 'I'm sorry it has worked out for them like this.'

Martha lowered her gaze.

I left mugs, milk and a pot of tea into the centre of the table and sat down myself. Martha looked up and I saw her bite down on that upsurge of rage and sorrow that has so frequently overtaken her these past few months.

I spoke to give her a moment. 'I'm sorry but I don't think you gave us your name.'

'Oh excuse me, my name is Faith.'

'Faith? That's an unusual name. You're the first Faith I've ever met.'

'I'd believe that, I've never met another one either. But my mother, she was a believer so that's where I got it.'

'She must have been one of the last.'

'I would imagine she was, she was a believer right up to the end.' She sipped her tea and cupped both her hands appreciatively around the mug. It was easy to imagine the small pleasure it brought with it.

'So when did you start your treatment?' I asked. It seemed best to get to the issue as quickly as possible. I could not see Martha holding out much longer. The room swelled with pent-up anxiety.

'I'm eighteen months into it now. My dosage has been ratcheted back from eighty milligrams a day to twenty, the side effects are much less acute.'

Martha was looking at her as if visual scrutiny alone could discern the psychological change in the woman.

'And if you are wondering, I can confirm that it has changed my life,' Faith went on.

Martha sat back in the chair. It was as much as she could do to not cross her arms over her chest in an aggressive invitation towards further explanation.

With a slight nod, Faith began to speak in a lulling monotone.

'I'd suffered from depression from my late teens. An incident – I won't go into it here – triggered an underlying depressive condition that ebbed and flowed to varying degrees throughout my twenties. And then, four years ago it hit me with such intensity that it swept the legs from under me and kept me bedridden for a full eight months. My whole life fell apart. Work, relationships and social life, the whole lot; I couldn't leave my bedroom or sometimes summon the will to wash and clean myself. During one of those hours of doomscrolling, which swallowed up so much of my time, I came across the trials that resulted from Elern's donation. They were looking for people to volunteer so I signed up to it. I fitted their profile – age, single and a long history of treatment. I am one of the first case studies, the last eighteen months under medical supervision. And so far' – she spread her hands – 'even if it doesn't work out in the long run and I relapse, I will always be grateful for the respite I've had these last twelve months. And that's why I'm here. Just to say a word of thanks. From the bottom of my heart.'

Faith seemed to instantly regret the redundancy of that last phrase and appeared momentarily thrown into confusion by her own misstep. If anything, it had the effect of underlining the sincerity of her speech as something that could not be argued against. She lowered her eyes to her cup; she had come to the proper end of her mission.

Martha subsided beside me, all the anger drawn from her by this pilgrim's testimony. It was probably only a momentary relief – those feelings were now too ingrained and deeply rooted to be swept aside by a few minutes' testimony, no matter how authentic it was.

'It was the time of year for it. The season of cheer and goodwill, I thought a word of thanks was the right thing.'

'And you thought you'd make a pilgrimage to the source of your own good cheer and give thanks.'

Faith smiled and nodded. 'My thinking didn't run so literally in that direction but yes, that does seem to be what I've done: a pilgrimage to the source.'

We let the statement lie for a moment. It seemed to take in more than her own personal predicament. I poured more tea all around.

It seemed wise for me to take my cues and tempo from Martha. Her reactions and emotions set the pace and direction in these discussions. It was a topic for another time as to why this should be – Elern was no less my child than Martha's and her tragedy was no less mine than hers – but it was understood between us that Martha's anguish was of a different cast than mine.

Martha clasped both her hands on her lap. 'It was here that we had our last discussion with Elern about the donation, at this very table. That was about two years ago.'

'Two, or two and a half,' I added.

'Yes, and it ended badly. I said something stupid and she stormed from that chair and left. The next time we met her she had undergone the process and she was in flying form, so happy with her decision to go ahead with it.'

'We should have known,' I said. 'Elern was always her own boss, always headstrong, she was going to do it no matter what we said.'

It pleased me to see Martha smile in recognition. Elern's wilfulness so often had them butting heads in the past that being at odds with each other was too often their default position. But now, in light of what had happened, it was easy to see all this as characteristic of courage and generosity. And if Martha had not yet gone so far as to interpret it as such, it seemed to me only a matter of time before she would do so.

Faith maintained a genuine interest in all our exchanges. It wasn't the forced attention of one who knew herself to be indebted or under obligation. Her interest was genuine and it was easy to like this in her.

And she wished to respond with some information of her own.

'It sounded so unlikely when I read about it first. This cohort of young women who could trace their family line back to a Famine poorhouse registry. And the whole science thing about those women carrying this magical enzyme in their limbic system.'

'Oh yes,' Martha said, 'and all the curative powers it brought with it.'

'Yes, as if this was history's recompense for what it had put people through.'

A complex weave of emotions passed over Martha's face. Something close to astonishment lit up her eyes.

'That's how Elern saw it too,' she said, 'That enzyme was history's gift to mankind. As a registered carrier, she saw it as her duty to step up and donate; history demanded it.' Martha lowered her eyes, difficult discussions now relived in her memory. 'That was our argument that night. I saw it as historical also but as something that needed further nurturing and safeguarding, not flogging off to some giant pharma corporation who were going to monetize it.'

'Is that what you argued about?'

'It was a part of the discussion all right, a difficult part. But what worried me was just how specific the ask was. I read all those announcements across social media about the appeal for any young women who could trace their lineage back to a Famine poorhouse – it sounded ridiculous, macabre and a crass misuse of science.' Martha looked her full in the face.

'And a big part of me thinks it's still ridiculous, no matter what evidence is put before me.'

Faith did not blanche. Whether it was some stubbornness that was native to her or she felt compelled to show she was worthy of Elern's gift, I could not say. Either way, she did not flinch from Martha's sorrowful anger. 'I can only speak for myself,' she said, 'And I can tell you that it has improved my whole life beyond anything I could imagine. That's all I'm saying.'

She spoke directly to Martha, giving it to her straight. And Martha appreciated this directness. Elern's gift would be safe with someone so blunt.

I left down my cup. 'A couple of days after that argument at the table I met her at a pub for a chat and a bowl of soup.'

Martha looked sharply at me. I carried on.

'It's a small place up the road and there was only a few people there. We were there about an hour when Elern drew attention to a woman sitting at a different table. She had been sitting across from a man, with a cup of coffee in front of her, which she had not touched the whole time she'd been sitting there.'

'A synth?'

'Yes, that's what Elern figured. Third generation also.'

'Those ones give me the creeps,' Martha said. 'The accuracy of their movements and expressions. I feel clumsy around them. It's like they have evolved beyond us.'

'Elern made the point that young and all as she herself was, she had a clear memory of a time when the possibility of such beings would have been considered something from the outer edges of the human imagination. Her broader point was that, in the presence of this synth, the idea of history seeking to redeem itself in this was not so outlandish.' I threw up my hands. 'But that's Elern, she's always had these sort of ideas.'

What exactly I hoped to achieve with that story I do not know, but I was aware that Martha was hearing it for the first time. Something about Faith's presence created the proper mood and context in which to share it.

'And yes, her idea did make some sort of sense to me when she put it like that.'

'It's a nice idea, but I have to say I don't see myself as the fulfilment of some sort of historical design. I just see myself as lucky and grateful.' Faith now appeared to think that her visit was at an end as she pushed back her chair. 'As I say, I came to say thanks. It seemed like the thing, especially as this was the time of the year. It was the least I could do.' She lifted her coat from the back of her chair.

Martha got to her feet and helped put her coat onto her shoulders. 'It's so unusual for anyone to mark Christmas now. My own memories of it go back to childhood with presents and family gatherings and so on. But even then it was a waning idea. So it's strange to hear someone talking about it.'

'As I said my mother was a believer, one of the last, and she celebrated Christmas with all the old customs of presents and family gatherings, the whole lot. I guess the mood of it rubbed off on me and that's part of the reason I'm here.'

The idea seemed to take her by surprise and she took a moment to tilt her face up to the light as if to test the truth of it.

'I will have a few friends around and give a few gifts. I might even decorate the house a little. My mother died a few years ago so this is my way of remembering her.'

Faith walked into the hall and opened the front door. Darkness had closed in and along the shore road the lights of neighbouring homesteads were visible.

I asked if I could drive her anywhere.

'No, I like to walk. It won't take long.'

She stepped backwards, and with a short wave and a smile she turned and walked off. We watched her go out the gate and turn left till she disappeared into the darkness.

Martha cleared the tea things from the table in silence. We both took a moment to straighten out our thoughts. I needed a drink and was lucky that there was a bottle of whiskey in the cupboard. Martha sat into the table and I pushed a glass towards her.

'I liked her,' she said. 'I'm surprised at that.'

'Yes, it was a relief to see that she was the sort of person she was.'

'It's a bit strange that she didn't enquire about Elern.'

'Knowing what we all know, I wouldn't have been too anxious to ask either.'

'But she was so direct. Why would she come here and not make any attempt to meet her personally?'

'Who knows how these people think.'

Martha was looking at me keenly, furrowing her eyes as if seeing something she did not like for the first time. 'You never told me about that meeting you had with her in the pub.'

'I didn't think it would do you any good. You were still in a flush of anger and fear.' I tried to hold her gaze. 'It would not have done you any good, none at all.'

'You should have told me.'

'I told you about the synth we saw, the woman with the coffee in front of her. But there was another woman also. An old woman, or at least she looked old. And she was all bundled up in a cap and scarf, she had tremors in both hands and blue skin.'

'Peccatum necrosis.'

'Yes, and the later stages of it too, judging by her hands. Elern said, "Imagine all the years that woman had to live through with people telling her that her illness was all in her head, that the idea of a pathogen crossing from the metaphysical realm was nonsense. All those years trying to make people listen before science validates her. And by the time that happens your health is broken beyond repair."'

'I don't understand. It was never inevitable that Elern or the other women would end up the way they have.'

'Elern's point is that—'

'I don't care what Elern's point is. You saw that woman, Faith. Full of light and cheer while Elern and that whole cohort of donors fade from themselves. Their memories gradually erased.' Martha's expression changed to a pleading disbelief. 'Their own names and addresses for Christ's sake! Their ages, the names of parents and siblings. The basic co-ordinates of their lives all draining away. Some of them are so far gone now they have stopped feeding themselves, they've forgotten themselves entirely.'

All the tension of the night bore down on her and she was now caught up in a mood of fist-clenching rage. Her voice narrowed down to a bitter sing-song, 'Hello Elern, how are you honey? My name is Martha and I'm your mother. You are my only child Elern and I love you to the moon and back.'

She turned to me. 'You don't have to make that speech, not yet, but I do. Every day for the past two months, like some scalding prayer.'

She lowered her face into her hands and gave herself over to deep, sobbing grief. And that terrible certainty at the heart of it would not allow me to put a hand out to comfort her.

Any day now it will be my turn. It will be my turn to fade.

GIVE UP YOUR INQUIRIES WHICH ARE COMPLETELY USELESS

Roisin Kiberd

There are no Christmas trees at the orgy. But they're everywhere else: standing in the living room of a New York apartment, against the wall of a doctor's office, and in a mansion's vast entrance hall. Christmas trees bear witness to this story, appearing in the background from the start until the final scene, in a toy shop, where the protagonist, Bill Harford, a doctor, shops for Christmas presents with his wife and daughter.

This is because *Eyes Wide Shut*, Stanley Kubrick's final film, is a Christmas movie, even if it isn't obvious. Its plot unfolds at the turning point between one year and the next, a time for celebration, both pagan and modern, but also reflection and retreat.

I first saw *Eyes Wide Shut* as a teenager, late on a school night, likely on Channel 4. I lacked the life experience to properly absorb it. I watched it for the orgy scene, which I'd heard about from friends, and the sex scenes with Tom Cruise and Nicole Kidman, which turned out to be fleeting and incidental (in this sense, these rumours echoed the marketing campaign, roughly a decade earlier, leaving audiences disappointed when the film didn't turn out to be porn, shot with a real-life Hollywood couple). As with Kubrick's *A Clockwork Orange* and *The Shining*, I watched *Eyes Wide Shut* as a yellow-sticker film – one labelled as strictly for over-eighteens and placed on a high shelf in Xtra-vision. This sticker was advertising in itself; it kept alive an air of danger, and defiance, experienced by past generations of Irish people, back when *A Clockwork Orange* was censored by the state.

I sought out *Eyes Wide Shut* for this illicit thrill, first in watching, then in bragging to friends about having seen it. Still, its strangeness got through to me. The stiff, passionless dialogue, in a film ostensibly about passion itself. The blue-toned darkness and saturated reds, spangled with Christmas lights, in Kubrick's hyperreal New York. The improbable plot, a night odyssey triggered by a confession, which unfolds like a somnambulant stroll through a half-remembered place.

Dream logic. I learned that term years later, in college, and knew instantly that it described this film. It doesn't make sense, on the surface at least – it works below that – and this is what makes *Eyes Wide Shut* hold up to repeated viewings. It creates a sense of interiority, of turning inward as the year ends. There's the infamous orgy scene at its centre, but before and after that there are night walks and lonely taxis, doppelgängers and masks, a stock-taking of love and identity and power, and, in the end, renewal and the promise of another year.

It is Kubrick's strange swansong, the film he called his greatest, a delirious dissection of sex and power. He died leaving us with something to chew on, on a quest for answers, just like *Eyes Wide Shut*'s protagonist, Bill.

On my undergraduate English course, for reasons never fully explained, we only studied the works of two film directors as part of a 'visual culture' paper: Terrence Malick and Stanley Kubrick. I wasn't taken with Malick – I knew that his films were beautiful, and widely respected, but I found them overly solemn, and drowsy. Why would I write about *The Thin Red Line* when I could write about the black monolith, or *Lolita*, or the Overlook Hotel?

Back in Dublin, on breaks between terms, I met a succession of film students, most of them male, who revered provocateurs like Michael Haneke and Lars von Trier. They made me suspicious. Being a film bro looked cynical and easy, an upgraded version of bragging about watching yellow-sticker films in school. You just had to find the least palatable, most miserable films made by audience-hating directors, and claim to love and understand their work in ways that none of your friends did. Kubrick, of course, was beloved of these types; he was an auteur after all, a man in absolute control, whose films called for detective work and theoretical duelling.

Had I not seen his films already at this stage, and begun to form my own ideas on them, it's likely that I'd have been put off Kubrick for life. There was a tendency in those days, the height of indie sleaze and irony, to cast a postmodern meaninglessness over everything, a wilful separation of experience and feeling. The result was that very little art was satisfying. We denied ourselves what was made to be felt.

It's only today that I feel close to watching *Eyes Wide Shut* the way the director intended, as something illogical that stews in the mind, exerting power through images and mood.

Kubrick's other films work this way too. Speaking to *Playboy* in 1968, while promoting *2001: A Space Odyssey*, he said, 'I tried to create a visual experience, one that bypasses verbalized pigeonholing and directly penetrates the subconscious with an emotional and philosophic content.'

There's a self-portrait of Kubrick, taken with a Leica IIIc at the age of twenty-one. It's an early instance of the 'Kubrick stare', demonstrated by its namesake. Several years into his early career as a press photographer, Kubrick sits at a table, holding the camera just below his face. It's a mirror image; everything is backwards, his head tilted slightly down, his eyes dark and alert, delivering not the dead-eyed glare of Jack Torrance or Private Pyle, but something more mysterious. Everything will follow: the plots and visions, the symbols and stories. Looking at this photograph, all I want is to know what's going on inside his head.

'If only you all knew,' says Albertine, the wife character in *Traumnovelle*, the book *Eyes Wide Shut* is based on.

But there's no way of knowing, not for certain. I'm a college lecturer now, and I can safely say that no interpretation is 100 per cent right or wrong, there are only convincing ways of arriving at one. Letting go of this certainty was hard for me as a student, but it's something I take comfort in today. And this is relevant here, because *Eyes Wide Shut* explores the themes of seeing and seeking and knowing. It forces us to make peace with *not* knowing too, in exchange for the thrill of partial discovery.

What situation, in real life, calls for having one's 'eyes wide shut'? What part of life makes this state not only preferable, but essential?

I used to be afraid of long-term relationships. I just didn't trust anyone enough. When men spoke of five-year plans and long-term intentions, I took this as my cue to leave. It is only now, in my thirties, that I filter *Eyes Wide Shut* through first-hand experience. I relate to this film differently as an adult, in the longest and most meaningful relationship I've ever had. Perhaps what makes it stranger is that we are both writers; we share that same conflicted loyalty to everyday life and to our work. Watching *The Shining,* for instance, there are times when I relate to Wendy, but also times I'm Jack (when in reality I'm probably closest to Danny, the disturbed child, now fully grown).

Eyes Wide Shut strikes me, instinctively, as a film about asking questions you don't want the answers to. It's about confronting what we *don't* know about those we love, and deciding whether we want to learn the truth, or remain in a state of wilful innocence, a marriage with eyes wide shut. While the film's turning point is the orgy, the emotional core of the film is the stoned, late-night conversation between Bill and Alice, in which Alice describes her fantasy of abandoning her family to run off with a sailor. This is what disturbs Bill enough to send him on his quest. In everyone he encounters – the masked women, the sex worker, the Lolita, the corpse – it is Alice's face he is seeking. For him, Alice stands in for all women, and she is projected upon with a familiar mixture of love and hate, reverence and misogyny.

I've never understood critics calling what unfolds between Alice and Bill an 'argument'; to me it's more like an exchange, or an inquiry. It's intense, but necessarily so, because both characters are trying (and, likely, failing) to get to the heart of something important.

Similarly, I've never understood descriptions of *Eyes Wide Shut* as 'distant' and 'cold'. Analytical, definitely. Cryptic too. It possibly reveals some deficiency in me that I feel more comfortable here, in Kubrick's world, than I often do in real life; an artificial place, where people don't ever truly see each other, and where every setting, event and person could be called a facet of the protagonist's imagination. I live inside my own head a lot of the time. I bottle up emotions till it's too late, and they explode into conflict. These are tendencies it's hard to hide in a relationship like Bill and Alice's, and like my own.

I write this essay from a small apartment in Neukölln, in Berlin, where Rob and I are staying for the summer. Kubrick might have enjoyed walking around Neukölln; it's a district where the paradoxes of the city at large are amplified. Religion, specifically Islam, is a visible presence in shops selling halal meat and modest clothing, but these sit side by side with dive bars and vape shops, their windows stacked with weed grinders and glass pipes. The day begins here with young mothers bringing their children to school, passing meth users at the

U-Bahn station. It ends with nightclub-goers meandering home, sharing the small hours with Middle Eastern, middle-aged men who bake *lahmacun* and *börek* for the morning.

Rob is in love with the Berlin night. As soon as we arrived, he felt the clubs calling. I'm more interested in yoga classes and gong baths and early mornings. We make our differences work, but it means that, some nights, he goes out without me, and I confront my fears about our relationship.

He leaves to submerge himself for hours inside Berghain, the pulsating cave of the city's subconscious, while at home, alone, I think about forces and people pulling him away from me; the things I try to forget, but cannot avoid. I hear the sirens outside and chew a melatonin gummy. Then I go to sleep, and travel into my dreams.

What does dream logic really mean? How does Kubrick capture the experience of dreaming?

In *Eyes Wide Open*, author and screenwriter Frederic Raphael ponders the same question, while drafting the screenplay for *Eyes Wide Shut*. Fragments of the book are composed as a film script, like this exchange with his wife, Sylvia:

> SYLVIA: I never did like dreams in movies.
>
> F.R: You know why they never work, don't you? Because the dreams that you dream don't have a *frame*, do they? Not like our vision, let alone like the frame of a picture or a movie … You're *in* a dream, not its viewer, *aren't* you?

You're in a dream and you feel your way through it, and, eventually, out of it. I know this from sleep paralysis, where I'll realise I'm dreaming but find myself unable to wake up.

Eyes Wide Shut is filled with unspoken oneiric details; Kubrick's New York is quite obviously fake, a soundstage built more like a memory than the city itself. It's all cobalt-blue night and crimson interiors, layering mood and intensity over oblique dialogue, spoken slowly, dazedly, with characters repeating lines back to each other as though in disbelief (near the end of *Eyes Wide Open*, Raphael is confounded when Kubrick complains that his dialogue is 'too good', and should be less natural – it is only in the finished product that we understand why). György Ligeti's piano motif, 'Musica ricercata', operates almost as percussion, the alternating E♯ and F♯ standing in for Bill's pounding heart, as dread builds and cycles in his mind.

This film is slow and heavy, with a plot that unfolds in its own time over the course of a night – perhaps the biggest clue that it takes place entirely inside a dream. We see Bill walking alone, people drifting into his path, then falling away while he continues on his journey (Kubrick used an old Hollywood trick for this, putting Cruise on a treadmill in front of rear-projected New York streets).

Then there's the subject matter, familiar to anyone who has dreamed of sex but found it oddly unsexy compared with real life. Sex spills out of this film, erupting in scenes where it does not belong. Women throw themselves at Bill, from Domino, a sex worker, to Leelee Sobieski's unnamed teenager, to Marion, the grieving daughter of Bill's elderly patient, to Nuala and Gayle, two partygoers who lure Bill to a place 'over the rainbow'. Money, too, does not reflect reality here. Bill spends extravagantly, more than even the best-paid, most sought-after doctor would, including paying Domino for her time even though they don't have sex, and infiltrating the masked elite by paying $200 over the asking price for a late-night rental costume.

Bill haemorrhages money, flashes his New York State Medical Board card, and in return doors open, beckoning him, and us, through without thinking. The reasoning for every action taken is dubious at best – why tell your partner a fantasy you know will hurt their feelings? Why make an illicit visit to a morgue? Why gatecrash an orgy, come to think of it, on the flimsy word of your friend, a rakish jazz pianist, and refuse to leave when warned by a masked woman that your life is in danger?

One of the biggest recurring details, in my dreams at least, is that I find myself in liminal places – elevators, schools, underground pools, long, Kubrickian halls – without explanation. Strange but familiar places, like Kubrick's New York. What makes *Eyes Wide Shut* eerie also renders it familiar to anyone who has dreamed. This opens onto the question of what we do with dreams. Do we interpret them? Sit with them? Take them at face value, as the truth about a shadow world in waking life?

Or do we bear in mind Alice's words, 'Maybe I think we should be grateful. Grateful that we've managed to survive through all of our adventures, whether they were real or only a dream.' Bill asks if she's certain, and she replies, 'Only as sure as I am that the reality of one night, let alone that of a whole lifetime, can ever be the whole truth.'

After the above, Bill responds, 'And no dream is ever just a dream.' The film is ending, but he's opening the plot back up.

How many of us can leave a dream alone, without interpreting it? How many of us have watched *Eyes Wide Shut* and felt as though Kubrick was speaking directly to the paranoid depths of our own minds?

Here's a list of theories, or dreams, or cultural hallucinations attached to his work:

> Kubrick faked the moon landing. He revealed this in *The Shining*, through coded messages including 'Room 237', the number of the soundstage he shot it on, and Danny's knitted 'Apollo 11' jumper; Kubrick shot *Barry Lyndon* with a lens originally developed by NASA to capture the dark side of the moon; *The Shining* is a film about genocide; *Eyes Wide Shut* is actually a documentary; in the scene at Ziegler's party, a pair of extras resembling Jeffrey Epstein and Ghislaine Maxwell, complete with dark bob and military-styled blazer, appear behind Kidman's Alice; the characters of Marion and Carl, who Bill visits on a night call, are doppelgängers of Alice and Bill; a second, invisible message is watermarked onto the paper handed to Bill at the mansion's gates; Stanley Kubrick died on March seventh, which is also my birthday, and seven is the number of diamonds featured without explanation in *2001: A Space Odyssey*, *The Shining*, *Full Metal Jacket* and *A Clockwork Orange*; Larry Celona, a journalist and consultant on *Eyes Wide Shut*, was also the first person to report the deaths of Stanley Kubrick in 1999 and Jeffrey Epstein in 2019; Kubrick was assassinated shortly after screening his final cut of *Eyes Wide Shut*, which included the 'lost sixteen minutes' in which he depicts the Harford's daughter being taken and murdered by a satanic paedophile cabal who also run the world; all work and no

> play makes Jack a dull boy; give up your inquiries which are completely useless; every Kubrick film examines power, and the powerful, and how power is abused.

Form is important here; form contributes to the mood and plot of each of Kubrick's films. At first I saw *Eyes Wide Shut* as a circular narrative, like in Arthurian legend, or *The Odyssey*. A problem emerges, and Bill leaves his home and journeys into the night on an adventure that will test his courage. Ultimately Bill does not triumph over the masked elite, but he wins an internal battle and his marriage survives. The plot resembles a circle, because it ends with the hero returning home (it's worth noting here that one early version of *Eyes Wide Shut* was to be shot in Dublin, with Woody Allen in the main role – an echo of the form and structure, and the Jewish hero of Joyce's *Ulysses*).

Bill is left with a sense of seeing but not understanding, and an instruction to return to what is familiar, like Dorothy in *The Wizard of Oz*, that other Christmas favourite, referenced several times in the film, including in the name of the 'Rainbow Fashions' costume shop. Nothing changes; that's the cruellest lesson Hollywood has to offer. Exciting things happen to rich people, and to superheroes, but not to you. You may have your escape, your entertainment, but in the end you will return home, and give up your inquiries which are completely useless, and live an uneventful life.

But *Eyes Wide Shut* is not circular; it's something even stranger, more eerily repetitive. Remember the name of Kidman's character, Alice, and Alice's journey through the looking-glass. The opening scene shows her looking into a mirror, while taking off her dress. Remember the plot: Bill and Alice are at home, then they go to Ziegler's, then he visits Domino and meets Nightingale, the pianist, who tells him about the orgy. Bill rents a costume from the Rainbow shop. He takes a taxi to Somerton, the mansion. He tears a $100 bill in half, and offers the other part to the driver when he returns.

At this point we reach the perfect centre of the film, at one hour, nineteen minutes and thirty seconds. The orgy begins to the sound of 'Backwards Priests', a reversed recording of Romanian Orthodox priests chanting the liturgy. When Bill is cast out of Somerton, he reverses his steps, beginning by handing over the other half of the banknote to the taxi driver. *Eyes Wide Shut* is a palindrome, a mirror-plot that plays forwards, then backwards. Bill dives into a dream, then returns to reality, waking before he can fully understand what's happened.

> Give up your inquiries which are completely useless, and consider these words a second warning. We hope, for your own good, that this will be sufficient.

I love the audacity of this message, handed to Bill at the gates of the mansion. It's like Kubrick, already known for cryptic detail, is telling us to stop trying to interpret what we're watching. It feels like an attempt to wind us up – we've just been given a masked ritual orgy, and now we're being told to stop thinking about it.

At the end of *The Tempest*, Prospero, the magician, throws his books into the sea. Kubrick signs off, from cinema and from public life, with Nicole Kidman's Alice telling Cruise's Bill that the only thing left for them to do is 'Fuck.' It's ridiculous, and true to form; Kubrick could not resist embellishing even his most ambitious works with a litany of dick jokes, much like Thomas Pynchon, who I'm starting to view as his literary analogue (both capture life at its most paranoid and profound, sharing a roster of themes including, but not limited to: war, power structures, technology, sexual deviancy, death and the ongoing nightmare of the American dream).

But before this, Alice tells him what Albertine tells Fridolin, the protagonist, in *Traumnovelle*: to be thankful for surviving these events, whether real or imaginary. I don't think it's as simple as what Dorothy says when she returns to Kansas, that everything she wanted was always in her backyard. Perhaps the truth is not that there's a secret society, but that Bill *wants* there to be one. Perhaps the response to *Eyes Wide Shut* illustrates Kubrick's point; the people who believe he was assassinated, or that the 'director's cut' is a tell-all about Epstein.

Our experiences change us. Knowledge changes us, for better or worse, even when that knowledge is not complete. Bill and Alice are closer now, and Bill feels more alive, having brushed with death. He has seen the Overworld and the Underworld too. He has revealed new parts of himself, by wearing a mask.

I suspect I'm not alone in finding that Kubrick's films satisfy the conspiracy theorist part of my brain. They conjure a sense of imminent revelation, the feeling of walking down a long, elaborately carpeted corridor, piecing clues together. His films are stagey and unnatural, but they create a sense of flow, an exchange of ideas that feels truer to life than cinematic realism.

It's something I enjoy, but try to keep in check, because I've seen the argument that Kubrick 'planned every detail' used to justify some fairly paranoid ideas. These are films about power, and powerlessness. They were made to mimic the feeling of standing at the foot of a simulacrum, feeling overwhelmed and a little suspicious. This is what makes them satisfying.

Watching *Eyes Wide Shut* today, I find it equal parts unnerving and reassuring. It presents marriage as a starting point from which its characters step into the unknown, before returning to each other. I find the idea of marriage daunting, even if I've arrived at what directly precedes it – a years-long relationship, in which we have both grown and evolved, but continue to love each other.

Few marriage vows attempt to commit the subconscious mind, along with the waking one. Perhaps, then, marrying someone means accepting parts of them you might never know or understand. Not admitting defeat, so much as acknowledging complexity.

Berlin is a city where a masked orgy might actually be taking place on any given night. I can't give up my inquiries – they might yet prove useful – but I'm trying to reserve them for art and not real life. To love someone requires living with what we don't know. This is where trust comes in; not a guileless trust, but one given consciously, with eyes open.

THE ANGEL OF LYON

Niall Bourke

I

I was asleep in the bedding store when Orlando burst in. His fringe, usually manicured, was plastered to his forehead in sweaty strips.

'Rupert, we have somewhat of somewhat of a … situation,' he said, stalking up and down in front of me with hands clasped behind his back. 'The Kenyan has really let us down this time; the Maasai dolt was meant to send me a gorilla. It should have arrived last night, by courier.'

'And it hasn't?' I said.

'No, it most certainly has not,' Orlando said. 'And, to compound matters, I've spent the whole week running up and down the stairs of festering French apartment blocks drumming up interest in its arrival. I've sold five hundred tickets for an unforgettable *Expérience du Jour de Noël!*'

'Just tell them to come back tomorrow,' I yawned, sitting up.

'It's an *Expérience du Jour de Noël*, Rupert. It has to be today.'

It was at this point I noticed Orlando had deposited a large and frumpy-looking sack into the corner of the store, and was now rummaging in it. He pulled out what seemed to be a dark and fluffy rug and, once it was free of the sack – no easy task – he held it out to me. It was shaggy and seemed heavy by the way it made his arms sag. Further inspection revealed it to be a gorilla costume. I sensed where this was going.

'Can't you just refund them?' I ventured, but without any real conviction.

'You've clearly never dealt with short-changed Gauls,' he said. 'Best avoided. Believe me. As miserly as the Franks, but lack the Lutheran restraint.'

'OK,' I said. I had my reservations, of course, but I'd found it harder and harder to say no to Orlando lately. It was something about the wine he provided each evening; it made me increasingly receptive to even his zanier suggestions. 'But only because it's Christmas. I'm *not* doing this again – no matter how much you butter me up.'

A smile ran across his flustered face. 'Oh, I knew I could count on you Rupert,' and he grabbed my ears, pulling me toward him and giving me a most slobbering kiss on the forehead. 'No more buttering, I promise.'

I took the costume from him and struggled into it under his watchful gaze. Once fully ensconced in the faux dermis I placed both hands on (now hirsute) hips and stared back at him.

'And …' he said, proffering me a fantastically realistic-looking mask.

'The mask too?'

'Of course the bloody mask too,' he said. 'What good is the bloody costume without the bloody mask?'

I put it on, fastening it to the suit by the seam in the neck. Then Orlando took my arm and led me outside and down a path, through a large and iron-barred gate and into the concrete expanse of an enclosure that had previously housed a pair of Siberian weasels.

'I'll be back to let you out at closing time,' he said snicking the key in the lock as he left, and I moved toward the bars of the gate just in time to see him run off towards the chinchilla experience. He stopped halfway up the path and turned around for a final time.

'And Rupert,' he added, 'just … just act … natural.'

And with that Parthian barb of wisdom lodged in my ear, I was left breathing in acrid wafts of weasel piss and wondering how in hell I'd ended up spending Christmas Day dressed as a silverback somewhere on the outskirts of Lyon.

II

Just shy of a month before this whole monkey business started, I had been studying at a prestigious art college in Paris and, although winter evenings sipping Châteauneuf-du-Pape in the fifth arrondissement weren't without a certain *bon charme*, it soon became apparent that my prodigious gifts were being wasted.

Not only was the place full of talentless mawks with all the originality of potash but – and worse! – my professors, having so evidently grown fat on the *foie gras* of tenure, failed to recognise the intricate subtleties of my work, even when it was left repeatedly on the doorsteps of their Montmartre apartments.

In truth I had long dreamed of a place where a *truly* avant-garde practitioner such as myself would be appreciated and, having now too long suffered the slings and arrows of artistic myopia, I knew I had little choice but to liberate myself from my Parisian cloister.

And so I lit out for Prague.

My plan was to spend the Christmas break pouring her famed festive and creative waters over my (by now well-and-truly parched) furrows and then set off to explore Bohemia; the *real* Bohemia, not the fake-glasses-wearing, oily-bearded-woolly-jumpered, fixed-gear-cycling-hipster abomination that seemed to choke the Left Bank like a plague of philistinish knotweed. But a misreading of both train timetable and bank balance saw me stranded at a station somewhere outside Lyon.

Well Rupert old boy, I had counselled myself on the platform, *you are now a limner indeed.* And with that there was but one option: to go seek out an establishment where such a weary artisan such as myself might wet a beleaguered whistle.

As I saw it, my best chance of success lay with investing the last of my meagre funds in getting drunk enough to strike up some kind of *entente cordiale* with a suitably visionary (and fiscal) patron of the Lyon artistic fraternity. But on entering the nearest bar, I remembered there is a certain *je ne sais quoi* about taverns near train stations: a seemingly inverse causality between the transience of the clientele and the standards of hygiene. And the dingy spit-and-sawdust in which I found myself was no exception. It was empty apart from a few ne'er-do-wells ferreted away in the corners, and a rotund barman whose sole concern was wiping dirt a bit more evenly around his beer glasses. I approached the counter and waited to catch his gaze. It was not forthcoming.

'Château Guiraud?' I ventured when he finally turned around, making an elaborate pantomime of uncorking a wine bottle.

He gave me a look of almost vegetable ignorance. A sommelier this man was not.

With reluctance I lowered myself to the naming of inferior grapes. 'Altesse? Pinot Noir?'

The last one he seemed to recognise. 'Ah,' he said, his portly face brightening, 'Wine, *non*?'

'*Oui, oui*,' I said. 'Wine,' and off he waddled, returning with a glass of plonk that smelled fit for stripping the enamel off bathtubs.

I was just starting to question the wisdom of parting with a (not insignificant) portion of my reserves for such refreshment when I heard the bats of a soft voice flap out of the gloom behind me, and I turned to see a brown-haired gent in a rather dapper three-piece ensemble sipping lazily from a glass.

'Not quite vintage, eh?' he said, doffing his drink in my direction, 'But needs must.' Then he deposited his glass on the counter beside mine and offered out his hand.

'Orlando Finch,' he said. 'At your service.'

III

It was clear from the off that our spirits were kindred.

Orlando explained how he had also liberated himself from the shackles of study – and at Oxford, no less – in order to go to Kenya and pursue his true passion: working with big game.

He was taken underwing by a Maasai chief and spent a number of years honing his skills before, for reasons still a little opaque, moving to Lyon to seek meaningful employment. And it turned out, in a turn of events almost as implausible as they were prodigious, that a Bavarian lederhosen magnate undergoing a fit of philanthropy happened to be opening up a string of low-cost petting zoos along the Rhône. Orlando's expertise had landed him the position as manager – but things were not going well.

'Rupert, the man is insufferable!' he had bemoaned to me across the greasy tavern table. 'He has all the vision of a mollusc. Goats and cows, maybe a few chickens at best. But no wonder the zoo is half empty. It's big game I need to get the crowds in!'

Here Orlando fell silent and began to stir his Riesling with his finger, but his balefulness passed as quickly as it had come on. He looked up at me anew.

'I say Binfield, now here's a card. There's a vacancy coming up. Mucking out stables and what not. I know probably not what you had planned but, with my expertise and your … creative leanings, I think we could convince that old Bavarian skinflint to see the error of his ways. What do you say?'

Admittedly, this was not quite what I had in mind when leaving Paris. But then the next round arrived and a brief foray into my emaciated wallet put paid to any lingering reservations because, while it is all very fine to suffer for one's art, actually suffering was a different matter entirely. So, raising my turgid approximation of wine I looked Orlando straight in the eye.

'Mr Finch,' I chirped, 'let's bring the bloody Serengeti to the Saône.'

IV

The job turned out to be better than expected.

Admittedly, the pay was both modest and irregular, but food was provided and I could sleep in the bedding store free of charge. The nights were chilly, but it was amazing how warm one could remain if there was enough straw down your trouser legs, and the work, as menial as it was, gave me much needed time to consider what direction the next run of my canvases should take. I even began to make some very promising sketches of jungle animals loitering in alleyways: vignettes that were simultaneously both urban and urbane. I did try to raise the matter of pay with Orlando, but he was very rarely to be seen during the day, always on some errand or other, and I was mostly left to my own devices: mucking out cages, hosing down enclosures, distributing feed and laying out straw.

In the evenings Orlando would resurface with a few bottles of wine and, after annexing one of the empty huts, we'd sit and enjoy dinner together and drink as much wine as could be stomached. And his overtures with the Bavarian lummox must have been working because, just two weeks after I started, we procured a lion.

I didn't see it arrive, but when I began my rounds in the morning there it was: a ferocious and awkward-looking brute with malevolent eyes, pacing up and down a cage that had up to then housed a family of Liberian mongoose. Orlando filled me in over dinner that evening.

'I finally managed to crack that bratwurst-fellating spendthrift Rupert. And the lion is just the beginning! If we play this right, we'll have the full safari experience here before the year is out.'

'Where did you get it?' I asked.

'I called in a favour from that Maasai chief, no mean feat I tell you. But for the love of God Rupert don't go near the feline fiend. He's as wild as the North Sea. Best leave the feeding and cleaning to me, at least until I have broken him in a little. Oh, and just to warn you,' he added, 'I'll need to start locking your door. Just for safety of course … in case he escapes.' And, to celebrate, Orlando produced a bottle of Rothschild out from somewhere deep in the folds of his jacket. 'And plenty more where that came from,' he said as he filled my glass, 'plenty more indeed.'

Over the weeks, the exotic lure of a lion proved too much for the paupers of Lyon to resist. The crowds grew steadily, so much so that we soon had long queues forming on weekends. Orlando was still absent from the early hours, but his bonhomie when he reappeared in the evenings was evermore indefatigable and, along with the Rothschild, bottles of Latour and Haut-Brion soon began to frequent dinner. Things were indeed looking up.

But I think he overextended himself with the gorilla.

V

Scratching myself through a prosthetic gorilla skin, I found myself in an animal enclosure on Christmas Day.

It was a large concrete bowl, ringed on three sides by a chain-link fence. The insides of the compound were sparse: a straw-bedded hut and a tree with a tyre swing hanging from its uppermost branch, a pile of bananas by its base. On the side of the enclosure sans fence, there was a low concrete lip that overlooked the lion's enclosure, and although I couldn't quite see the lion from where I was, I could hear the Nemean brute had woken up and was now pacing up and down as is the unhealthy habit of such beasts when kept in captivity.

Seeing a pile of browning bananas by the base of the tree, a rumbling started in my stomach and reminded me I'd missed breakfast. I knuckled over to the tree, picked up the most edible looking of the bunch and started to peel it – and here something wholly unexpected happened. A cooing began, soft calls of, '*Regarde Maman, regarde*,' began drifting, and not unpleasantly, across the enclosure and in through the seams of my costume. I turned to find a crowd pressed against the fence and all pointing in my direction.

Now being naturally introverted, it had been my plan to simply sit in the hut until I was released that evening. But seeing the amassing crowd it occurred to me that doing so would be a grave error. As an avant-garde practitioner, I had here a unique opportunity; not only could I make a mimetic comment on the irony of man's inner animalism, but I could also *simultaneously* deconstruct the erroneous assumption of a dichotomy existing between the real and the performed. And so, after eating my banana to a round of applause, I stood up and started to beat my chest, elucidating a further astonished murmur from the crowd.

Buoyed by the reaction, I knuckled back and forth across the enclosure a few times with a renewed vigour, emitting the odd *oo-oo* as I went and then, after treating the crowd to another pectoral pummelling, decided to really give them something to talk about over their cassoulet that evening.

I aped with aplomb over to the tree trunk and began to scale it with as close to simian dexterity as could be mustered given the cumbersome restrictions of the suit. Here, the crowd really started going wild, and I felt their fervour mixing with the remains of last night's Haut-Brion. It was, I'll admit, a little intoxicating. I sprang from branch to branch, each successive leap greeted with a louder cheer than the last until, as if being carried on the crest of one of the breakers of applause that were now crashing onto the enclosure, I made one final and audacious jump for the highest limb so I might pivot around the trunk and finish up my performance with a bow from atop the tyre swing.

But midway through the air I realised something: there is, and despite my earlier existential wranglings to the contrary, a distinct difference between pretending to be and being. Down I crashed into the lion's enclosure with an unmerciful thump, landing on a pile of straw as the shrieks of impoverished French infants punctured the air.

I lay on my back, patting myself down for broken bones. But no sooner had I started to count my blessings for such a soft decampment than a guttural growl brought me to my senses.

There, not twenty feet away, was the abominable beast of a lion.

It was standing stock-still and staring straight at me. Slowly, it sank back onto its haunches, coiling like a spring as its eyes became coals. For a frozen moment I watched the hackles bristle on its neck – and then it pounced, covering the ground between us in terrible, sinuous bounds before descending upon me like an avalanche.

'Help!' I yelled, 'Help!' tearing off my mask as I prepared to face down the throat of imminent feline decapitation.

But imagine my surprise when, instead of trouser-despoiling roaring, I was met by something else altogether. Enfeebled German mutterings coming out through the mouthpiece of an uncannily lifelike lion costume.

'*Bitte*,' the lion whimpered into my ear as he pretended to rip out my jugular. '*Bitte, um Himmels willen, setz deine Maske wieder auf. Bevor wir beide gefeuert werden.*'

VI

When they finally uncuffed me in the interview room, the *gendarmerie* confirmed there *was* a lederhosen magnate. He was called Herr Schnuber. But he was from the Tyrol, not Bavaria. And Orlando hadn't been *working* for him. He'd been his lodger. Until, that was, Orlando had drugged Herr Schnuber's Pilsner and locked him in his own coal house.

Then, the detective told me, Orlando had done something quite unsavoury to get Schnuber to hand over his bank details. I didn't quite follow it all, but it seemed to involve an earwig. Orlando had emptied Schnuber's account, using the money to buy a derelict zoo in Lyon and a pile of animal costumes from a bankrupt Biarritz film studio, before finally herding the poor man into a pig trailer and driving him to France.

'What can you tell me about this?' the detective said, sliding a piece of paper across the interview desk. 'We found it in Mr Finch's 'otel.'

It was an old magazine clipping.

Devil's Breath

Few drugs are as foreboding as 'Devil's Breath'. Known scientifically as scopolamine, this little-known drug from South America has been linked to numerous reports of mind control and induced 'zombie-like' states of victims whose drinks have been spiked.

I read it open-mouthed. I'd really tried to give Orlando the benefit, what with him being an Oxford chap, but I had to admit it. It did seem he'd been a bit of a cad. 'So that's how he got us to dress up?' I said.

'*Monsieur Schnuber? Oui, certainement*,' the detective said. 'But you?' and he gave one of those Frenchest of shrugs, raising his eyebrows and blowing air out of his pursed lips. 'On that, we are still investigating. And about this?' he said, sliding another piece of paper over to me. 'I take it from Mr Finch's not book.' It was a page with a list of animals on it. Beside each animal was written some notes.

Lion = Herr Landlord
Gorilla = ~~Must be able-bodied but desperate~~?? Rupert, mon dieu!
Leopard = Dear old pater … it's been a long time coming.
Zebra = A must have! But will need two. Must work well in tandem. Siblings?
Chimpanzee = Small man? Amputee?
Armadillo = Child. But how to shorten the legs?
Giraffe = hmmm …

This time it was my turn to shrug at him, albeit apologetically.

The detective turned to his partner. '*Pas impliqué*,' he said. '*C'est un imbécile*.' He turned back to me. '*Merci Monsieur*. You have been most 'elpful. You can go.'

'Thanks, old bean,' I said. 'Thought for a minute I might be batting on a sticky wicket.'

'And Monsieur Binfield?' he added.

'Yes,' I said.

'*Joyeux Noël*.'

LITTLE CHRISTMAS

Maggie Armstrong

It was nearly midnight when they got off the tram, hidden deep in woollen overcoats. Brigit sped up the path and Jacques followed; where, he wasn't sure. Neither of them knew where this thing they had begun was going to end but the cold was stupendous. Minus three, with a frozen Grand Canal and east winds that just felt cruel. Was he walking her home for her safety? Or for his advantage? Recently she had begun to realise that every man she'd ever met had been a fraudster. That their common element was *her*, and that *she* had orchestrated every problem.

They were back on the subject of the film as they crossed under the tram bridge onto her deserted street. Bitter January wind blanched their faces and she gripped herself, crumpling closed her gloved fingers.

'Emma Stone was alright, but I don't think a French harlot would take that much pleasure from her work.'

He slowed his step and looked to her to elaborate, but just then an icy blast whisked her coat around her body and lifted up her hair, spraying it around her head in a wild halo and sticking strands to her lipstick. She pressed it back behind her ears, embarrassed. Earlier she'd been so contained she reckoned she'd fooled everyone.

Not that he'd made any effort to divest himself of his mystique – the French mother, his three children, the job. They had been colleagues during her brief stint among the office population, though they met in playgrounds these days, then at a mince-pie affair a month ago. After that the texts, erratic but sustaining in December. This had been her idea, once she'd had confirmation of his divorce, and neither of them could say the evening had gone badly.

They'd met in the pub across from the cinema at 6pm. He had picked an Oscar-nominated movie. Three hours of subtitled pornography. He had placed on the bridge of his nose a pair of black-framed spectacles, and it seemed he couldn't bear to look at her even once. The restaurant had gone on for hours – a bottle of red wine, fish platter to share, espressos, house truffles. Then to another bar for a nightcap. Gin and tonic that froze the centre of her chest as she sucked up the last rasping drops from the ice cubes.

They had sat having yet another conversation. He couldn't get to the end of a book – she couldn't get past the beginning, not since her daughter. 'The words are scrambled, and the characters and plots, it's not nice,' she told him, and he still didn't brush her calf with his though it was right in front of him. The music was too loud and everyone was much younger than them. She couldn't tell why neither of them suggested leaving, but it was like an invisible thread had wound them lightly together, and there was nowhere else that they were meant to be. His eyes sparkled and she looked back at him with sweet, amenable invitation and just a little scheming coquetry, or so he picked up, he couldn't be sure.

They got outside and were immediately stunned with the cold that had been forecast, and they had to go quickly, somewhere.

The street flashed a metallic blue as they neared her doorway where the narrow, battered pavement edges tapered to the ground. Glancing back at him, she pulled off a glove and felt around her pockets for her house keys.

The nice thing to do, of course, would be to just invite him in. But then she had to remember to never be nice again.

He was inspecting doorways and the treetops on the next street over. His eyes were wide, benign, with something shrewdly elsewhere. His face was pale in the lamplight and the way he stood, he took up very little space, seeming to disappear from the very perimeters of his own self. To suggest it in outline, in quick glimpses, without fully disclosing who he was.

'Well it was great seeing you—' he said.

'It *was*!'

This came out wrong, much too surprised. She liked flirting, always had. Company made her interesting, and she was amazed at her stamina when it came to the retailing of a witty story, the same one she'd told someone else. But this part, saying goodbye, it caused confusion, distress practically. It ate up moments she could not afford to lose. This was her free weekend, her only time without Miranda clutching her and shouting, '*MAMMAY!!!*'

She fitted her key into the lock and elbowed her way through, one foot still on the doorstep. It wasn't that she wanted him to come inside. It was that she didn't want him *not* to. She didn't want to see him walk away.

'Do you want to come in? For a nightcap?' They'd had one already. 'Another nightcap,' she clarified. 'If you want?'

'Oh, I don't want to keep you up.' But he followed her, untying his scarf and shutting the night behind him.

The hallway was lit with a bare, dangling bulb, damp black leaves scattered across shining white tiles. 'This place, it isn't very nice, sorry. There's no coat hooks but anyway it's too cold to take off your coat.'

They passed the pram tucked under the stairs, its blue hood turned up, and coats precariously heaped on a hall table. Envelopes and sheets of paper spilled off the coats to the floor, and onto shoes. A mud-caked wellington, a patent red Cinderella slipper, a pair of black sequinned ladies' boots.

She knocked a weathered purple scooter to the side and pushed open the glass-panelled door, chattering. 'So cold! It's like an igloo in here but come in.'

Jacques tried, as in every house he'd ever entered, to appear totally uninterested. The strip of kitchen, for example, didn't ask to be seen. A loaf of grey-coloured bread had been left out on a breadboard, with butter, jam, and a torn packet of Tesco Swiss cheese. Tipped sideways onto the gas cooker, something with raisins crumbled out of tinfoil.

He was struck, amazed even, by the commotion in the room. The walls had been scrawled with lines and circles, patches of blue and yellow and black, and cloudy smudges. There were toys and jigsaw pieces spread across the floor, markers everywhere. Colouring books, a scattered deck of cards. Next to the sofa were books in jumbled stacks. Children's books, with battered covers, and novels, one he had even heard of.

By the hallway door, a black sack bulging thick with clothes, maybe intended for a charity shop. He had one like this by his front door as a matter of fact, though he hadn't overfilled it. She needed two bags for that.

Brigit plugged in the tree lights and a triangle of golden baubles came to life. The star on top was cut from paper, and dead needles lay scattered in a ring around the floor. She toured the room, moved a handful of mugs into the sink, then went and grabbed hold of a radiator and recoiled, quivering. 'Are you frozen? The heat should come on, but those radiators aren't filling. It's another problem.'

He really didn't mind the cold, he told her, hands in his coat pockets. He went to the back door and peered out, and a circle of condensation filled the glass with his breath. The neighbouring redbricks tilted high above them, with two or three rooms dimly lit. A shadow passed one of the walls and Jacques retreated from the window, aware the two of them could be seen.

By the tree she had the ironing board laid out, with a basket of crushed clothes balanced on top, a shirt sleeve trailing off it. Lately, on a Friday when Miranda went back to her dad's house, Brigit carried the basket in from the broom cupboard and propped it on the ironing board, and every Sunday when Miranda came home she stuffed it back in the cupboard with its pile not reduced. She never wore her shirts, so let's not bother, she'd conclude. Miranda left every fortnight for the weekend and Brigit was ashamed by just how much she loved those precious days alone.

She opened cupboards, and took down gin, black rum, a thick remnant of crème de cassis, and tall glasses with snowmen printed on the sides.

'What's your poison? Spirits, glass of wine? Campari? Tea?'

'What will you be having?'

She screwed open a bottle and peered through the neck with one eye. 'What about a hot port?'

'Delicious. Thanks, Brigit.'

She started, thrilled to hear her own name said aloud.

'Where did you get these?' he asked, examining the base of one. 'I actually need cups for the kids.'

'Oh they're TK Maxx.'

'Are they stackable? I must look for some. My tableware has really suffered in the past few years.'

She nodded, her back to the cooker, eying him. *The past few years*. That was how he'd been labelling it. And would he, like earlier, smoothen down the details of his marital collapse and move carefully to another subject? He was just another fraud, another psychopath, surely. But his manners were so good, he was impossible to read.

As the kettle came to the boil she felt an old ache in her shoulder blade, and she ran her hand around her left index finger, bandaged since Christmas Day. Her only lemon was stuck to the fruit bowl with blue mould, so she threw it in the bin and sliced up a clementine. She took down cloves to stick into the slices but stopped, and stared into nowhere.

The act of doing things for someone else suddenly bothered her enormously. It dazed her, with a sense of mild disaster, as if the glass might drop from her hand and smash all over the tiles. She yawned, loudly, and scattered the cloves in loose then pitched in the slices. She'd liked the restaurant better. The leather seats, the waiters, being served. She thrust his drink at him without meeting his eyes.

'There's some of my mum's Christmas cake, if you want. It's mostly marzipan icing left, Miranda picks it off.'

'Oh no, thanks. I couldn't.'

They carried their hot glasses to the sofa by the window-sill, and she rearranged the cushions and brushed them with her palm – they were scattered, he noticed now, in a confetti of sprinkles. 'Rainbow sprinkles,' she explained. 'We were making gingerbread men, Christmas Eve, she got hold of the tub. Sit yourself down!'

She drew in a long sip of the port and looked brightly at him.

'It's strange you are here. Isn't it?'

'Well, I hope it isn't too strange.'

'Not at all, no. Just that, I haven't really had like friends here, since everything.'

He wondered. Was she going to keep saying *everything*, or would she just tell him what he was getting into?

'It was a newbuild, but they hadn't finished building it, and it had been sitting for a year by the time they let us rent it. There was dust all over the floor, and thistles out there taller than me, and thorny branches. I wanted it so badly I told the estate agent, *Oh, I'll pull out those weeds, I love weeding*. I begged a man to let me weed. Sorry, these are a little heavily spiced.'

He swivelled his drink and sipped it, staining his lips dark pink. 'No, delicious. I don't think I've drunk this much since, I don't know, the year 2000?'

'Oh I was twelve in the year 2000!'

'Sure. Twelve?'

'Twelve. Happy New Year.'

They drank, and in the glass, she saw themselves, their watery reflections, the drooping tree. Tomorrow she could look forward to unstringing the lights, boxing up the decorations and dragging it out of the room. The branches were turned inwards like long black claws. Perishing before her eyes since the middle of December. She worried, lately, that no living thing stood a chance when it came near her. Everything she touched would break or start to die. She felt for him, being here with her.

He put his glass down on the rug and sat back. 'So you convinced an agent you should have a house that was way below your standards. What happened then?'

'We rented it empty, completely bare. It had none of this. Like, light fittings, those shelves, kitchen table. I got an Exceptional Needs Payment and unleashed the money all over Homebase. But we've trashed it, haven't we?'

'Oh, no, it's very homely.'

'There were no beds. No wardrobes. You know what gets to me? The way you assemble the wardrobes – basically, I put my friends' husbands to work – you assemble the things and find you haven't ordered knobs to go with them. So there I am, the baby strapped to me, high-tailing it up to the hardware shop for fucking knobs. You know what? I can't pass a hardware shop without shuddering now. Though I did purchase my first tape measure last year. Miranda snapped it immediately, playing tug-a-war with her friend. And I learned to use a hammer and nails. I feel so tired.'

'Oh – dear. I better let you get up to bed.'

'No, I don't mean literally tired. I have very little interest in sleep, the opposite, I can't sit still, since everything. It's like there's always something preying on me, from inside. Another vital task, or someone I have forgotten to reply to. Some unpleasant dealing with Miranda's dad.'

He nodded, then sat up facing her. 'Would you like to tell me what happened? You don't have to, but if you want.'

She drew in all her breath and looked sorrowfully at her fingernails. 'If I told you, you wouldn't believe me. You'd think I was inventing it.'

'Oh, Brigit.'

'When I try telling people, I feel like I'm making it up, like I'm lying. But I'm not lying, I mean I wish I was. For my daughter's sake. But you know what? I don't even feel sorry for her. She's doing fine. Isn't that horrible? I feel sorry for myself. I must be depressed. I can't look beyond my own anguish.'

She sprawled next to him but felt very aware of herself, her muscles softening out and her curves flattening the cushions. The quiet swelled around the room and just being there together seemed gruelling to her. The drawings looked much harsher, more chaotic with an audience. She was conscious of the life she had allowed spawn around her, the disarray. Miranda had seemed to her a genius when she'd drawn those first quaint circles, but what she once thought was endearing now looked irresponsible. She coiled her legs up differently, and her knee knocked onto his. But neither of them moved, as if obediently waiting for some instruction.

'That's a nice dress you're wearing.' He picked up the hemline and held it out in his palm.

'Thanks, it's a skirt.'

'Oh. But it's lovely, I noticed the pleats, when you walked up to me earlier.'

She swallowed the end of her port and winced, then flung herself back on the sofa. 'You know I had to sell all my clothes, after, everything? In a crazed effort to make space in our suitcases!'

'Oh gosh.' He let her skirt go and sat up.

'This is the first time I've got to sit on this sofa throughout the holidays.' She held a blue sprinkle between them, then blew it away. 'Do you not just feel exhausted all the time?'

'Well, you must be. There's a lot on your plate. And then,' he whistled. 'All those soft furnishings. That would be the end of me.'

She turned to face him, glowing with mischief. 'I bet you've got power tools. I bet you know how to use a Phillips head.'

'A Phillips head? No one would be unable to use a Phillips head.'

'You would have been so useful to have known!'

'It's a simple tool. You would have no problem. Oh Brigit.' He stroked her hair. 'I wish I could have been there.'

They were so close that if she moved an inch she would fall into his arms.

Get him out the door and sleep on this, she thought.

Don't proceed, he thought, *not now*. But then, he didn't want to leave her either. He'd like to take that dress off, definitely. Even just to feel her bare skin against his.

He hadn't brought anything, probably for the best. He wasn't sure how capable he would be at this hour – whether this was just a game for her, a story to tell her friends. She was still talking, this time about her father, how she missed him and craved firesides. They were so alone so much of the time. Did he not feel just so alone?' She laughed, but composed herself, her eyes lowered with a barely comic gloom.

'Brigit. What can I say. You're doing a wonderful job with your daughter. Look at her. She's so creative!' They looked around them, at the pictures stuck with Blu-Tack, the ghost-like wisps, a spray of glitter by the tree.

'Seriously it's like the Lascaux caves in here,' he went on.

'Frescoes – actually it's a tourist attraction. I'm going to start charging visitors.'

He slung an arm around her. She dropped her head on his shoulder and he pulled her close. Resting her eyes closed, burying her face in his chest, she breathed in a flowery laundry powder mixed with sweat.

She thinks I'm about to try and kiss her, he thought.

He thinks I'm about to lunge, she thought.

'Listen,' she said, drawing away. 'I don't want to hurt you. But I will. I cause damage, everywhere I go. Unfortunately. I have a nasty streak.'

He shook his head at this, and as if in panic, she hid her face again in the dark of his sweater. He pulled her close, running his fingers through her hair and she hoped he would take command of the situation when he asked her, 'Should I head off?'

She blinked up at him. 'Is it late?

He took out his phone.

1.22am Sunday 6 January

'It's Little Christmas today.' She looked at him excitedly.

'So it is.'

'That's what my mother calls it. People call it Women's Christmas too. Nollaig na Mná. When the men—'

'Nollaig na mBan,' he corrected.

'Nollaig na mBan, when the men are supposed to do the work and the women relax, that's the tradition. We never had it growing up. My dad just did his share of the housework.'

'I mean, as he well should have. But it's still good to hear.'

'That's how I remember him, cleaning, gardening, doing things. He was very much into equality and dividing the labour. So I'm not convinced we need a special Women's Christmas. What is it telling people? If we put our feet up for one day only, are we also accepting that we kill ourselves through December? Sometimes, there's no choice. I had a rubbish Christmas! How was yours? We haven't talked about Christmas.'

'Mine was a lot of work, but I loved it.'

'Mine was work. My account went into overdraft. I gashed my finger on an onion.' She raised the grubby terracotta bandage of her left index finger. 'I got calloused hands. Miranda screamed at me. She was sick for a whole week. Strep. And cold sores. Her Baby Annabell doll needed batteries, and one of those tiny screwdrivers. If I'm honest Christmas was overall dreadful. Was yours dreadful?'

'No, I mean, it wasn't that bad. Santa Claus came and filled the stockings, the kids were delighted.'

'I guess they would have been. But were you able to share in their delight?'

'I was. I don't get to spend as much time as I'd like with them. So it really is a joy for me, now they are past the difficult age. It goes quick, you know.'

The room was quiet, and cars scraped the streets outside, the wind drumming on the windowpane. He took her hand in his and he kissed her bandaged finger, once, twice, then held it to his lips. She was breathing softly, gazing up at the ceiling. She thought he might say it was time to leave when he sat up.

'Can I do anything for you, before I go?'

She eyed him. 'What kind of thing?'

'I don't know, but you're so tired. Miranda is coming when?'

'Tomorrow,' she said sadly, desperately. 'Tomorrow she'll be back.'

'Just while I'm here then, I don't know, help?'

'You think this place is a disaster, don't you?'

He laughed, and the lines that flicked out from his right eye gave him a look of overriding kindliness.

'But you're completely right, it's a disgrace here, just at the minute. Do you like ironing?'

She'd been joking, but he was already standing, sweeping sprinkles off his clothing, straightening his belt and cuffs. He took off his coat and draped it on the sofa back and she watched, suspicion on her features, as he filled the iron with water and plugged it in.

'OK. Let's clear a path first, all these crayons can go somewhere, and the dolls.'

She put her legs up on the sofa and reached for a book at the top of the nearest stack. A novel, bought for her thirteen months previously. She opened it but contemplated him.

Carefully, he picked up a shirt, and then another shirt, a pair of trousers, skirt, Miranda's festive red frock, crushed into a stiff ball, like a rose. He seemed to be flattening each garment, examining the laundry labels before making separate piles. It looked, if she had to guess, like he was making a system.

She laid her head on the cushion and kicked out her feet to get more comfortable. Hot steam gasped from the iron and each smack it made was soothing to her. It meant jobs underway, industry, the sound of another person working on her behalf. He worked quickly through the piles, not perfectly, she noted. Beyond the window, the last light of the house went out and darkness cloaked the yard. She couldn't keep her eyes open and things and people returned to her like stills from a movie. A French harlot in the throes of ecstasy. A velvety black crow standing on a green postbox, its beak clamped like the blade of a knife. Then her father, his back to her at the sink with an apron tied around his waist. A woman on a sofa smoking a cigarette in long crackling drags.

Miranda, coming home, throwing her thick arms around her mother's neck and pressing her warm face against hers.

Every so often, she heard his voice.

'Will I keep going?'

'Oh yeah, if you'd like.'

A little while later, 'Shall I leave you?'

'No, no, not yet, stay a while.'

Words she couldn't make out anymore. Her name again, whispered this time. 'Brigit.'

'What's that?'

She shook herself and opened her eyes, pretending to be wide awake, to see him holding up a piece of silk. Her nightdress, the colour of melted butter, lost at the bottom of the basket this past year or so. 'Isn't this too delicate? Unless I covered it, hold on.'

She sat up and looked around the room as if they were elsewhere. She could see it again, the shiny floor with nothing left on it. He'd moved the book stacks, and she spun around to see their glasses drying on the draining board. She took him in with a surge of wonder, observing him with awe, framed by the wall, his shoulders jutting out in a diagonal line as he stretched and cracked his back. Two stacks of ironing sat tall in the basket at his feet. The golden nightdress fluttered in his hands and he laid it on the board.

'I'll give it the lightest blast, will I?'

'Oh yeah,' she drawled. 'Blast away.'

CHRISTMAS TRIFLE

Arja Kajermo

In the Intensive Care Unit she had been quite a star. She had been Exhibit A. The brain surgeon was well pleased with her and introduced her to the class of medical students. 'Look at her! Sitting there taking notice two days after her craniotomy!'

He wasn't praising her. He was boasting about his skill with the scalpel.

But her Exhibit A days were soon over and she was sent to a public ward. It was packed with rows and rows of beds. The patients seem to be octogenarians and centenarians. Some slept with their mouth open. Others slept with their rheumy eyes open. There was a sound of gentle snoring. Some were wandering around talking to themselves, like an army of walking wounded going nowhere.

'Is this a geriatric ward?' she asked the nurse who had come with her from the Intensive Care Unit.

The nurse said, ‘No, those that were well enough were sent home for Christmas to free beds for the elderly from nursing homes. Other oldies were dumped in the A&E by relatives who couldn’t cope with them over Christmas. Happens every year!’

‘Really? I want to sign out from this … bedlam! Can I do that?’

The nurse picked up a pillow from the bed and plumped it up furiously. ‘That wouldn’t be wise! I have to get back to ICU now!’

The nurse hurried out.

The patient called after her, ‘Happy Christmas!’

The nurse looked over her shoulder and said, ‘Get well soon, pet! And Happy Christmas!’

She sat down on the bed and felt drained. Not Happy Christmassy at all. Was it the drain from her head to the container pinned to her hospital gown that was sapping her strength? She studied the container. Was she losing grey matter?

She looked in her overnight bag and found the notebook where she had written down a description of trepanning: ‘A trepanning is perforation of the cranium by drilling or chiselling a hole in the head to treat problems related to intercranial diseases. A skull from 7000 years ago was found in a cave in France. It seems the patient survived the procedure and lived for a few years after it.’

She had looked it up in the library before her operation and had kept it because it could come in handy for something to talk about. In case she had visitors. So far there had been only one visitation but it was a big crowd who threw their coats on her bed on top of her and talked amongst themselves for an hour. And then shuffled out after their impromptu, premature wake.

She went to the bathroom to look at herself in the mirror. Her head was shaved on one side. On the other side her hair was hanging long and limp. Not a good look. The crude stitches on the bald side of her head made her look like Frankenstein's monster. A nurse had suggested a comb over and she had asked the nurse to shave it all off. But the nurse had just giggled and said hairdressing was not part of her job description, and walked away.

When she found her nail scissors she went to the bathroom and cut off the offending long bit of hair. It took forever and she left a mess of hair in the handbasin. Her self-administered haircut gave her the look of a newly hatched chicken. Or one of those women who had been given a punishment haircut.

Back in the ward she changed into a clean nightdress of her own, not one of the hospital ones that were open at the back. She put a cardigan on to hide the 'wound-exudate container'. The word 'exudate' gave her the shivers. It sounded disgusting.

Ward Sister walked by and said, 'Oh, all dressed up and nowhere to go!'

'Thanks, Sister! You bitch!' she mouthed without making a sound.

A student nurse came and told her that she and the other student nurses had organised a Christmas Day dinner for tomorrow. Did she have any special requests about the food.

'Are you a vegetarian? Any allergies?'

She said she wasn't able for Christmas dinner. Could she be excused?

'Of course you can't be excused! You have to come! We're making such a big effort to make Christmas Day special!

Everyone in the ward who is able to sit up at the table has to join. Only the bedridden patients are excused! We are putting up decorations and there will be games and crackers! And there will be sherry trifle!'

The nurse looked pleadingly at her.

'Well in that case! I love sherry trifle.'

The next day she was hurried out of bed and marched by two sturdy nurses to where the Christmas dinner was laid out. There was a big serving platter with turkey and ham already sliced up, there was stuffing and a sauce boat (with what could maybe be lumpy gravy), there were boiled potatoes, cabbage and two (small) jars of cranberry sauce. There was even a forlorn-looking Christmas tree decorated with balloons. Balloons?! That's a new one. Shouldn't it be baubles? Balloons are for a child's birthday. Then she remembered it was Baby Jesus's birthday.

The oldies were wheeled in with their Uribags swinging on stands with wheels. But who was she to sneer? She, with the box with grey matter pinned to her chest. They were all in it together. The student nurses served up the dinner. A loaded plate for everyone. They turned a deaf ear to those who said, 'Just a little for me.' Hardly anyone was able to finish their portion. So their plates were collected and the desserts were put in front of them. She couldn't smell sherry in the sherry trifle. It was a mere sponge with red jelly. She wouldn't even pick up the dessert spoon. She hoped the nurses wouldn't hold her down and force-feed her the jelly. She wouldn't put it past them, now that they were on a roll. Big strapping girls they were. Used to subjugate farm animals.

She made to stand up and muttered, 'Can I be excused—'

But not a chance. The student nurses pushed her down on her chair and told her it was time for the crackers. She was given one end of a cracker to hold and the nurse pulled the other end. The cracker snapped open with a bang. And a whimper from her. A paper hat and a comb fell out of the cracker. What was she supposed to do with a comb? Turn it into an instrument? If you fold a piece of baking parchment around the comb it makes a sound a bit like a harmonica. The nurse put the paper hat on her head.

Next! The nurses howled like a pack of hyenas. One of the old dolls was picked to pull the next cracker. A nurse came over and closed her hand over the old woman's trembling fist and helped her pull the cracker. A paper hat and … a key ring! And so it went on and on until they all had paper hats on their heads like court jesters. There was a pile of every kind of useless object on the table: a pencil sharpener in the shape of a duck with the sharpener up its bum; a red pencil with a rubber at the top; a plastic ring; a whistle thing; a badge that said *Kiss me quick*; and more.

Now she made her second attempt to make a run for it. She didn't make any excuses, she just stood up and walked away and got to her bed and got in and pulled the blanket over her head.

The Ward Sister came by and asked her had she enjoyed the Christmas dinner, and was she expecting her people to come and visit during the holidays. She stuck her head out from the blanket and said it was too long a journey for them and they couldn't get away from the farm and the milking. Could she make a telephone from the Nurse's Office to her family? Since it is Christmas? Please?

Ward Sister said she would think about it. Patients were not supposed to make private phone calls from the office, she said and walked away swiftly. Her soft-soled nurse's shoes didn't make a sound. Only her starched uniform rustled faintly. Was that a big NO?

'Happy Christmas!' she called after Ward Sister, who just kept walking. She didn't look back.

FEAST OF SPARROWS

Sue Rainsford

I needed to speak with my mother. She was hard at work basting meat in the garden where the morning – part steam, part dew, already fading – had settled around her.

Our family had a taste for pinker game, but this fat bird had been slain especially for Christmas Day. My mother had mounted the spit the night before, had been readying the carcass for days. She had undone the fact of its feathers and worked her fingers into its every dark crease. Into those soft places had settled butter, salt, garlic. The wet zest of a knobbled lemon. And she had sung to herself, while she worked. I was still young enough to believe the dulcet chords played some role in keeping the meat tender.

It was a sight reserved for Christmas Day, my mother's strong arm rotating the fragrant flesh on the spit while it gathered the honey-slow glaze.

The garden before me and the parlour behind me with its own fire roaring in the wide grate. The house was warming by slow fractions because it was a house made, mostly, of stone, and the stone held onto the cold. The cold was like a clean and shining blade and, like a blade, it made short work of your throat. That slicing feeling: was that the reason I was taking so long to call out to her?

The sparrows had been loud in the trees all morning. *They do not approve*, I thought, *of us feasting upon this other, larger bird.*

When I told my mother what I had to tell her, I'd have to raise my voice over their high chorus.

And what did I want to tell her?

I'd almost forgotten, I was so taken by the sight of her. That, and I was a child. A child on Christmas morning.

'Mama,' I said, 'there's a man at the door.'

My father and sister were on the Christmas hunt; we were in the very last moments of the morning, so they'd be back from the woods in an hour or so.

My mother and I, alone.

Or at least, we had been until a few moments ago when I heard a knock and knew, by its quick metre, it was someone I'd never met before.

Does it ever bode well?

A strange man at the door with the dwindling morning behind him, asking, 'Is your mother home?'

He seemed easy enough in his own skin and he'd a certain heft inside his furs. He looked nothing like my father, which is to say he'd a fine set of cheekbones and eyes that took their lead from the light, were quick to flash olive and hazel. When he turned in the doorway, he caught the early noon sun on just the one side: they might have been the eyes of two different men.

Two different men, and both of them looking for my mother.

Now I had one foot on the parlour rug and the other on the patio's moss-clung stone.

My mother said, 'Come again?'

Like I say, the morning – it was so cold. But my mother had already been hours at the fire, she'd left her furs folded inside the parlour door. The sweep of her bicep as she managed the spit and the ladle. Her chest with its own sweaty glaze.

'There's a man at the door.' A folded wing rose up to meet her. 'He says he knows you.'

But *was* that what he'd said?

There had to be a reason I had come back here, that I had chosen to distract her rather than tell the man to go.

'Has he a package?'

Something relating to the dinner, she meant. But everything had been delivered in the days before.

I shook my head, and she tweaked the spit so the whole, sweltering bird rose up an inch or so. Its plucked flesh shook when it settled and there was, now, a clear ring of panic to the sparrows' tune.

The scent of the cooking bird had spread over the garden which was thrumming around her. The knotted hedge and the constant oak.

She put the ladle in its copper pot.

‘Strange time to be calling.’

‘He has green eyes,’ I said.

I think she knew, then, but she had no time to recover herself.

He was standing behind me, having let himself in. I remember it, the rage I felt: now my mother would think a man at the door was something I could not handle. She'd think I'd offered him this view of the tree and the ornaments fastened to its branches, of the gifts littered with the needles those branches had shed.

He hadn't seen her yet. He was at the fireplace, looking at its high mantle that held a single photo of my mother in her wedding dress.

‘For the love of God, Daniel.’

When he turned, when he saw her – those green eyes went wild in his head. She might've been a rushing bull. A creature led by its rogue heart and the desires flashing red inside it.

‘Annabel.’

When her name came off his tongue it was a sound I hadn't heard before.

It had the hush of a prayer but the heat of something else.

It was a single pour of velvet.

No, it never bodes well. A man at the door, trailing the cold and the first pale shafts of noon. The fire picked up the lighter strands of the pelt around his shoulders and those strands in turn picked up the almond flecks in his close-cropped hair.

He sat down in the fireside armchair.

‘You've had children,’ he said.

My mother was wearing a smock and she'd undone the top buttons. Her collar, where it met itself: that was where her sweat was pooling and that was where his eyes landed again and again.

'I did, and their father will be back soon.'

'How soon is soon?'

'An hour,' I said.

She cut her eyes at me and I knew, too late, I shouldn't have spoken. I thought an hour would put fear in him. I didn't understand that an hour is plenty of time for all sorts of things to happen.

'An hour,' he said from the chair where my father had sat while my mother set the fire beneath the spit that morning, telling me to pour a glug of whiskey in his coffee.

It is Christmas, after all. He'd squeezed my hand, the hand which wasn't squeezing the neck of the bottle, and tossed the hot liquid down his throat. Bent over to lace up his boots. Sound of my sister readying their guns in the hall. Outside, the fire was making steam of the frost.

Yes, it was Christmas. But now something was happening that had not happened before and I'd seen no hint of it all through the traitorous morning.

My mother turned away from him. I thought, *She cannot bear the sight of him in Father's chair*. But she was looking at the meat – she did not want it to be ruined.

I watched him; I watched him watch her body. The place where my sister and I had grown, that soft part of her which had spread around us and retracted unto itself again. The improbable magic of organ and tissue that had left its silvered latticework across her low belly.

I still feel you there, she sometimes said, and – barely, *barely* – the latticework breathed open.

'And you?' She turned around, interrupted his gaze, 'Did you have children?'

He laughed, cast his hands over his knees.

'No.'

Of course he was a single man if he was roaming around on Christmas Day.

'Where have you been living?'

And he named a place three towns away.

'And you,' he said, 'you stayed.'

'Yes,' her eyes moved to the mantle, 'I stayed.'

She looked over her shoulder again, and this time went outside. I thought, *She has left me alone with him.* The sparrows picked up their frantic song when they saw her, loud enough that I heard it all the way from the tree line, heard it over the crackle of the two fires. I watched her baste; that strong arm, its steady rotation. She was as sure as the tide, or that deeper, oceanic pull which sets the tides in motion.

Into the blended sound of the sparrows and the fire he said, 'You look a lot like her.'

Which was not especially true. My sister was the greater likeness; glossy shock of black hair, a particular slant to her shoulders.

'She looks like her father.' She was standing where the heat of the parlour and the cold of the garden blended in the slipstream of the open door. 'You might put some wood on.'

And he did so without getting up from the chair, reaching for the basket by the grate. With his face turned away I thought, *This is her chance. She will tell me to run away.*

But he leaned back, asked, 'Little one have a name?'

Fanning herself with the smock, my mother glanced at me. 'Maude.'

'Maude,' he said, 'I'm Daniel.'

She looked over her shoulder again.

'What are you doing here?'

He nodded at the tree, our gifts beneath it.

'It's a sentimental time.'

'And that's how you're feeling, is it?'

'No, I'm feeling angry.'

'And why are you angry?'

She said it with a sigh, so I knew it was a question she'd asked him before.

The wood he'd held spat back at him; a spark landed on his furs and he watched it burn.

'You may as well have a cuff around your ankle,' he said, and swiped the hot little nugget away.

'Because I'm cooking a bird on Christmas Day?'

They spoke as though the sparrows weren't every moment getting louder. My eye kept tugging toward the garden where they shook the thinner branches of the birch. Over that constant sound, he was asking, 'Do you like your life?'

'Always the great inquisitor, Daniel.'

And she stepped outside again.

I thought, *I'll run into the woods and find my father.*

But he turned to me, said, 'What age are you?'

'Seven.'

'Seven's a very lucky number.'

'I'll be eight soon.'

'No reason eight can't be lucky, too.' And then, watching her come back towards us, 'Those damn birds.'

'You can hear them?'

He made to answer me but now my mother was back and her chest was shining afresh; skein of sweat between the twinned bones of her collar. A small moon that would upturn if those two bones ever met.

'Right, time for you to go.'

'Are you having many over?'

They'd spoken at the same moment and neither wanted to be the first to speak again. You will say I saw it because she was my mother and I will say it was there to be seen by anyone with eyes in their head.

The whole of my mother's body: it fluoresced.

She caught the light like the nacre of an oyster recovered from some ancient rock bed, and this man had come because to him her gleam meant something else, something he believed he was owed because it was Christmas.

My mother leaned against the settee, pressed the back of her hand to her cheeks. She cast about the room, saw her own young face on the mantle.

How can they talk like we're not standing in her singular glow?

'Ten,' she said.

'Ten!'

'All my husband's side.'

'And he,' he looked to the fire, looked back at her again, 'is he—'

'Daniel, you have to—'

'Mama,' I said, 'I don't feel well.'

And it was the truth. My stomach had made a dash for my throat. My mother's hands were on my shoulders and I felt the edge of the settee against my legs. I clutched at her, said, 'I can't see, I can't see.'

Because while I could feel my lids glossing over my eyes I saw only a black and endless shore. She laid me back and rearranged my limbs, said, 'Open your mouth.' And down my throat went the honey-rich glaze. 'You need sugar.' To him, she said, 'She's had nothing to eat all day.'

Where the glaze had touched my lips they were sticking together. I could smell it, the browned sugar of the honey. I could smell the Christmas tree and the cooking bird and the fire that was working through its flesh and this stranger's furs warming as he sat in my father's chair—

I retched, and the glaze scorched my chest.

'Your only job,' my mother said, 'is to take another breath.'

I must have slept. Her hand was gone. Weight of a damp cloth across my lashes.

On one side of me, the light of the fire was jerking. On the other, the doors opening onto the garden were a lambent almost-square. There was a swathe of shadow between them, and this shadow danced before me.

That darker portion of matter; it beat like the wing of a bird locked, by its own confusion, between a roof and its rafters.

For all its frenzy, it was going nowhere.

The movement was constant.

Perpetual, self-enclosed.

And all the while the sparrows chirped their protest at the slaughtered bird whose meat was surely ruined, whose coal-black flesh was surely, right this moment, falling away from itself.

The charred specimen that was to be our Christmas meal.

The meal we dreamt of all year, the prize meat slain at the peak of the season, at the moment its flesh was ripest, its breast succulent and firm.

My father had brought the bird home from the woods. He'd taken it into the pantry and left it there for my mother – lain it on its side. There was blood on his sleeve, and he took off his shirt there in the pantry. Small corridor of a room and there was his body, its simple bulk. He handed the shirt to me, and I got to work. With my two hands I held the cloth beneath the kitchen faucet and watched the water do its rivulet work while my father, going up the stairs, called out, *We might even have snow.*

The whole time, the bird was losing its heat in the pantry.

And Mother, my mother – she had let it go to ruin.

My father and sister would be back any minute and my father's family thereafter and we'd have to feast on blackened cartilage and salted ashes while the smear of smoke in the garden rose up and up and up—

The sparrows were vicious in the trees. I wanted to cover my ears but the shadow before me had ceased to move.

I waited: I watched it.

It seemed to breathe, a slumbered beast.

Or it might have been the pulse to my vision.

I did not know what the shadow meant, but it meant something – didn't it have to mean *something* – that he had heard the sparrows too.

And then, my mother's voice.

'The meat, the meat—'

I sat up and the cloth fell away.

My mother stood at my feet with her eyes on the garden, watching the bird that had only grown more tender, whose flesh would fall away from its bones, the bones we would suck so as not to lose a drop of flavour. There was not one part of this animal we would not taste.

He was sitting by the fire that took up the grate as it had before, and now he slid his eyes toward me without moving his head. I knew, but could not put words to it then, that he looked at me the way he did because he saw me as strange kin.

We both had an unshareable knowledge of the same body.

I had some grasp of every woman's warm interior. Which is to say, I understood there was a place in women where men might go. A place they begged entry to, and where they submitted themselves to an unforeseen blend of joy and penance.

I did not know how bodies locked together, but I knew there was a sacred darkness in my mother and that it was linked to the tenor of this man's voice when he said her name when he first came into the room.

Annabel, Annabel.

Two women in the room, and only one of them my mother.

Only one of them had put her hands on me.

Only one of them cared whether the meat spoiled.

And, the other. The other—

The sparrows; they'd shatter their own beaks. Their little throats would be raw. Their song speckled crimson and only themselves to blame for the blood-spatter over their nests.

My mother's eyes were still on the meat. Her hip beneath the coarse smock, the slip of her shoulder. The chest she could not seem to keep cool but that she carried on fanning nonetheless when she said, 'Three hours away, Daniel. That's where you've been living.'

Again, she took a step toward the back door. I could see the mist coming to curl against the invisible wall which was the heat of this room, of the fire and the bodies before it.

'Do you remember any of it?' he said.

She brought her hands up to her eyes, then; a quick and startled reflex. Shielding herself, too late, against a hurt dealt here and now in this room, or else a decade ago. When she looked back at him her eyes were smudged with the fire she'd been tending. Coal and ash, ash and coal.

'Stand up,' she said, 'stand up.'

'Annabel—'

And she made a sound I'd heard her make at the tomcats and foxes who prowled the dusky garden, a kind of whipping sound from the back of her throat.

When she made that sound, he moved back in the armchair, and he lifted himself up –his cheekbones and his eyes and his sparkling furs – as she thrust her chin toward the front door.

After we'd heard the door close.

After I checked to see if he'd tread in any telltale soil.

After she'd readjusted the spit.

After the fire had been stoked.

Only then, I stood in that hot-cold place between the parlour and the garden, and said, 'Mama.'

She was on her knees, the meat level with her face. 'Yes my girl?'

She did not need to tell me he was a secret. He was like the knocked bottle of milk on the countertop, unnoticed for hours during which it forever altered the careful grain of the wood. He was a bloodstain on my bed sheets that looked like a fresh-kill spoor, scoured in the dawn bathtub. He was simply another thing my mother and I had tended to when no one else was home.

'The sparrows,' I was running out of words. She looked up at me, waiting. 'They're so loud today.'

'Are they?' She picked up the copper pot, tilted it. 'Maybe they're nervous.' She moved the pot closer to the fire so it would soften the glaze. 'The frost makes it hard for them to find leaves for their nests.'

'But the leaves are dead.'

'That's right.'

'They shouldn't use dead things for their babies' nests.'

I was talking just for the sake of it, just to hear her voice and have her prove she was still herself word by word.

She was turning up the cuffs on her smock where they'd unfurled. She was adjusting her knees before they began to ache upon the stone. She had yet to clean her face, and so when she spoke to me it was from behind that partial veil of ash and coal.

'The leaves get warm when they decompose.' I blinked at her. 'They give off heat as they rot.' Over my shoulder, into the parlour, she said, 'Sometimes only dying things will do.'

I didn't know how to answer her, so I put my fingers to my own eyes, to show her where she was marked.

She touched her face, looked at her grey fingers.

Looked back at the cooking bird.

And then my father and my sister were home.

The others would be arriving soon and the fire was low enough that my mother had pulled her furs back around her shoulders. My father went out to her and my sister showed me the creature they'd killed. You could tell it was young by the tight slope of its hips: it had yet to moult, had not yet bred.

Over the spit, the bird's sweet-smelling skin was crackling.

My father and my mother were talking low. He'd a hand, now, on her hip. Now on her shoulder. The place that had been bare hours before, when she'd been too hot for her furs.

When my father's family came in the door their eyes and mouths were glinting.

'We're starved!' My aunts said, tidying their swept hair.

'Yes, starved!' said my cousins, knocking their booted heels against the doorstep.

My uncles shed their furs into a heap in the hall, their nostrils flared.

Their quick eyes and their sharp teeth.

'We're starved, Annabel!'

The table in the long, good room was set. The curtains were pulled back from the high windows and I sat where I could watch my mother. This deep in winter the sky was quick to give up the first sliver of moon and so it was under a hint of that pale planet my mother carved up the bird.

Yes; now, at last, she'd taken a blade to the meat.

On my empty stomach my father offered me a sip of wine and my sister laughed at the face I made. She tossed her whole glass back and my aunts, my uncles, my cousins, we all of us laughed with our mouths washed a grainy crimson.

Outside, my mother kept carving.

I could not stop looking at her, how she moved. I couldn't stop because I wanted, so badly, for her to come inside. I wanted to sit beside her.

And, also, it did seem – in that wilted sunlight, under that partial moon – that she was tearing away slices of her own succulent flesh.

Even now, as she came towards the house with the plate held against her chest, the meat did look to be falling, falling with every step, from her own sweet and bloodied breast.

The sparrows; had she ever heard them?

The family had taken up their knives.

'Eat!' my mother said, with one foot over the threshold, 'Eat!'

And we, with our wet eyes and our red mouths, we fell upon her.

We *could not wait* to fall upon her.

No wineglass chinking.

No fireside crackle.

No sparrows – no, no sparrows.

Only the pant of our hot breath.

Annabel, Annabel.

Hush of prayer.

Pour of velvet.

Dying things, you'll find, hold heat for a long time, but when at last the meat was gone my mother was very still in her chair.

I watched her, and I waited.

I am waiting. Every Christmas.

Mother, my mother.

I wait for her to move again.

CHRISTMAS NUMBER ONE

Soula Emmanuel

'Jennie Barrett has a lovely broach from Switzers,' she said. 'Silver and purple. She's going steady with a fella from Booterstown and he bought it for her.'

'Jennie Barrett is the height of glamour,' I said.

'That she is!' Gran replied.

I didn't know who Jennie Barrett was – a former work colleague, probably, back when Gran worked in a factory making clothes – but I enjoyed the old lady's stories, the way she sat on her leather sofa like a guru and rattled off photographic details about scenes long past. The anecdotes oscillated around a conclusion that never quite arrived, and then she would say, 'Is today Saturday?'

She thought every day was Saturday – but when you're an old-age pensioner, it sort of is. Her lapses were entirely forgivable.

It emerged slowly, like a shadow that coloured her but did not yet threaten to take her away. She poured milk over her cornflakes, but put them in the microwave and there I'd find them hours later, limp and curling. But the errors were cumulative. She started losing weight. She became frail. She aged a decade in only six months. When the shadow took her, the bed kept her.

Putting her in a nursing home was harder for us than it was for her. It was a grand, pale-blue building, an old manor on the edge of town with a glass porch over the front door. My mother promised to make sure someone visited her every day. 'Don't make such a fuss,' she replied. No matter their age, there is no one lonelier than a child without parents. Mum didn't want to lose the counsel, or the authority, or the outmoded, constabulary parenting advice, especially now.

'At least she's a widow,' my mother would say. 'She doesn't have a husband depending on her,' attempting to obscure how reliant daughter was on elderly mother.

For me, it was one less person to tell. I wasn't good at telling my family. The words would roll around in my mouth and fall limply to the floor. *Mumble, mumble, hormones, mumble, mumble, gender.* Where did it all lie in the hierarchy of announcements: was it like a new job, or an engagement, or a terminal diagnosis? Did it need any hullabaloo at all?

My friends thought I was nuts. Over gin and tonic they'd tell me, 'You're a big girl, Evie. You can do whatever you want. Just tell them, and if they have a problem with it, it's their issue and not yours.' But for me, family was something I was adhered to – like one of those humane mousetraps that isn't humane at all, because by the time the mouse is found it's gnawed its leg off trying to get away.

Not everyone knew. I hadn't formally come out at work – some of my colleagues were vaguely aware, but I hadn't gone all the way with human resources. I was *boymoding*, as it were. A horrid little term; if it was merely a mode, I wouldn't have had a problem with it in the first place. To some, I was Evie, and to others, I was something else.

(Not Stevie. Wash your mouth out!)

It would be a weird Christmas this year. That's what everyone in the family said, and boy did I know it.

I had always liked the social rituals of the season – the old decorations, the €5 Kris Kindle at work, putting the song from *Snoopy* on the home-sound system on Christmas Eve and keeping it on repeat for hours – but in my first year as Evie, I didn't know what I was doing. More to the point: isn't Christmas all about giving? Isn't it about other people? I didn't feel very festive, wrapped up tightly in all that personal drama, busy labelling myself instead of my bountiful gifts.

It was Gran's first Christmas in the nursing home. She would be well looked after; I kept being told that by my mother, as though to hush a suspicion, though I never doubted it. The guests at the home – they are called guests, like it's a hotel – would have their turkey and ham together in the afternoon. They would sit around big tables like attendees at a wedding. They would listen to Nat King Cole and pull their crackers and have a wonderful time, so much so that they probably wouldn't notice their families' absence.

But something about it gnawed at my mother. 'We need to make sure she remembers who we are,' she said. 'Friends of mine had parents in nursing homes during Covid – they all forgot who their relatives were in lockdown. The only people they saw for months were the staff, and they all wore masks. They forgot how to interact with people. Non-verbal communication, reading facial signals, recognising a smile. It was the beginning of the end for them.'

The solution, she decided, was a family portrait. Not just us, but all the cousins, all the children and grandchildren, so a picture of us all could sit on Gran's dresser in the nursing home and never be forgotten. And that meant that I had an announcement to make, to a swathe of my extended family.

My younger cousins all knew. It was only their parents, my aunts and uncles, I needed to inform. Suddenly I felt an acute bravery welling up in me, like mulled wine simmering on a stove. I texted them one by one. I just told them, *I am transgender*, like I was telling them where I was waiting to be picked up.

Some of them replied by telling me that they had already figured it out from hints dropped by my mother, or that their kids had told them. Or they would reply with a thumbs-up emoji, the calling card of the aloof and middle-aged, like my decision was one they were fundamentally jaded with. But then an uncle, Liam, replied by asking if I was planning to tell Gran.

You shouldn't tell her, he wrote. *It would only be confusing for her.*

I was a little bit furious. Confusing for her? It was confusing for damn near everyone, even for me, but that wasn't the point. At the end of the day, it was only a picture. We weren't planning to test her on pronouns or make her watch *Drag Race*.

But there it was: a veto, or something like a veto, which hung over me. Perhaps he was right. I decided to pack two bags of clothes for the photo shoot. A large one with make-up, the works, and a smaller one with my boymode.

An appointment had been made for us at a photo studio in the depths of the southside, off a neighbourhood of huge detached houses watched over by the Dublin Mountains. There were hugs and kisses in the car park. It was only October, but that didn't suppress a certain festivity in the air, the atmosphere of the last day of school, everyone relaxed and a little merry.

I inhabited the moment like a bit of thread coming off a jumper. My aunt Marcella looked at me forlornly, because I wasn't dressed as Evie. 'Whatever makes you feel comfortable,' she said. 'Don't worry about today, Evie. Just get through it and then life goes on.'

'Are you sure?' I replied. 'I don't know what to do.'

That elicited a vague annoyance in her, because she didn't know what I should do either, and she wasn't about to take responsibility for it. 'I don't know,' she said. 'Just do what makes you happiest,' leaving me feeling batted away. That was exactly what my mother had told me earlier in the day, when I asked her how I should dress for the shoot. People may be good at telling others what to do but sometimes they really excel themselves at washing their hands of you.

Inside the building, the corridors were all exposed white-painted brick and cheap carpet that smelled funny, the sort of thing that made you feel you were behind the scenes of a concert. We were introduced to the photographer, a short man with a tidy dark beard called Leo.

He asked us why we were there. My sister, Tara, twenty-years old with a brown bob, launched immediately into the story of Gran and her dementia, how she was now in a nursing home, us wanting to make sure she remembered us. Then, there was a glimmer in his eye as he said, 'Of course, I knew about your grandmother, I just wanted to see who was the chatty one, and now I know it's you.' He nodded towards Tara and she gave him a headlight stare.

Is all of this really necessary, I wondered, looking through my two bags of clothes on a wooden bench in the changing room. Does a photography session really need to prod so deeply into our souls? Does it need to be a psychological root canal of secret games and hidden analysis? Can't we just say cheese and be done with it? I had a vision of this taking ten minutes but Leo seemed to have plans for us.

The two sets of clothes looked like the palettes of two completely different paintings: one a dull landscape, continuing off indefinitely, with nothing much to say for itself; the other a vibrant but confusing modern work that has something to say, even if nobody fully understands it.

Then Tara came up to me. 'Are you mad?' she said.

'Why would I be mad?'

'You can't dress in those old clothes for this. You'd never forgive yourself.'

'Uncle Liam said it was best not to confuse Gran.'

'You're not going to listen to him, are you? Don't worry about what other people want. Gran would respect it. Or she would, if she was a bit more with it.'

'I just don't want to impose.'

'Evie, Gran lives in a nursing home. She has Alzheimer's. Most things confuse her. The fact that I'm not still in primary school doing finger paintings for her confuses her. Don't be a martyr.'

'I'm not being a martyr,' I said, 'I'm being considerate.'

The studio itself was blindingly white, empty but for a scattering of uncomfortable-looking Ikea stools. There was a toy chest off to the side, and the younger children and their parents went off to find something to play with, to create the illusion of candour, so that for a few minutes the room was a muddle of jangling metal rattles and wooden cars travelling across the floor.

I felt out of my body in that moment, the way one might going through a job interview, having learned off rote answers. I looked at the camera when it was asked of me. I sat on the weird stool. I smiled, widely, with my teeth. I was doing a perfect job. I was doing what needed to be done.

I was a brilliant grandson.

I didn't have a toy to play with, like the children did, but I might have appreciated it, the distraction. I would have preferred to disappear into a group but here I was, in all my glory, being photographed alone. I could only get through the experience by clearing my mind – but then, my mind seemed to come back to me, utterly full of thought and exasperation.

'Can we … can we pause this?' I asked.

'Sorry?' the photographer replied.

'Just … I need to change into a different set of clothes. I'll be, like, ten minutes at most.'

'Yes, of course, go ahead.'

And I ran, even though I had no good reason to, back to the dressing room, back to my two stupid bags of stupid clothes. The feeling came back, the one I had been successfully avoiding for so long in the studio. Shame. All I wanted to be was myself, yet being myself seemed inevitably to represent an imposition on other people, the kind I had spent my whole life up to that point avoiding. It seemed a cruel joke the world was playing on me, like I was caught in a hamster wheel of my own emotions, never getting to any kind of resolution yet perversely convinced that I would get somewhere eventually.

Now, though, was different. The shame didn't stop me. I had got to that point and I wasn't about to turn back, so I put the clothes on. Tights and flats, bra and blouse. Necklace and make-up and something approximating a smile. I was ready to go out. I felt like I was preparing for combat, like a boxer about to be called into the ring while their signature tune played.

I wondered what my song would be. I imagined Chaka Khan and put aside all thoughts of Aerosmith.

Yet when I entered the room, there was little reaction. A young cousin was crying, and people were waving rattles in her face to entice her to come around. Nobody was looking at me. Until Tara caught a glimpse, and let out a strange kind of applause.

'Yes, here's Evie! So good to see you again.'

The photographer said he had photographed transgender clients before, and reeled off a list of names of local queer notables I had not heard of. Then he thanked me for being fully present at the photo session.

'Now we will get to capture the real you,' he said, and I smiled, and almost said, *Yes*.

Here I was, in all my glory.

Christmas Eve was infused with rain, the kind that stuck to everything, that left the wooden floors of the nursing home squeaky and treacherous. Some of the family were to go to Mass afterwards; others said they would go on Christmas morning, but everyone knew they were lying.

Our full complement gathered to present Gran with her present, pushed into a side meeting room draped unconvincingly with tinsel. We were given half an hour by the staff, because this is the twenty-fourth and the other guests have family too. I sat perched over the edge of a cushioned yet hard wooden sofa, probably an antique.

'A big crowd,' Gran said. 'What's the occasion?'

'It's Chriiiiistmas,' a cousin said, like Noddy Holder.

My mother took the picture out of its cardboard box. It looked like a series of mirrors, each reflecting a different face back, like a video-game screen where you could choose which character you wish to be, the kind of world I might have craved at one time.

'And who is this for?' Gran asked.

'It's for you,' Aunt Marcella replied.

'For what?'

'For Christmas. It's Christmas Eve.'

'Is it?'

'Yeah. That's why we're all here in our jumpers.'

'And who is that?' Gran asked, pointing at a small child in the corner of the frame.

'That's me,' the child, Ava, responded.

'Of course it is. That's very good of you. You're so kind.'

Then Tara stepped forward. 'And that's Evie, there, your granddaughter,' she said, pointing at the image of me. 'Doesn't she look wonderful?'

Gran looked at the picture with a studied consternation, like it was a map she was trying to decipher. 'Yes,' she said, eventually. 'She looks beautiful.'

HAPPY, AND FULL

Briana Fitzsimons

'I need the—,' the woman gestured to her own shoulder to demonstrate to the butcher exactly which part of the pig she needed to buy a chunk of.

The man behind the counter with the blue eyes and kind smile laughed as he mimicked her. 'You want the shoulder. Got it,' he said, his thick Tallaght drawl rolling over the fluorescent-lit meat display that stood between them.

The woman nodded, unconvinced. 'I need the skin on, bone in.' The nasal sound of her American accent harshly contrasted with the lyrical tones of the Irish voices around her in the butcher's shop.

'Whatever you want,' the butcher shrugged. 'Why would you be needing that anyway?'

The woman smiled, but kept herself small. 'I'm going to slow roast it. With lots of garlic.' The man scrunched up his nose in disapproval. 'I need to pick it up on Christmas Eve. Will that be alright?'

'It's for *Christmas*?' the man asked incredulously. 'No *turkey*, no?' The extra vowels he added to the word 'turkey' made her pause for a moment to make sure she had understood him correctly.

She shook her head, her long dark curls bouncing with the movement. 'Just the pork shoulder. Thanks.'

The butcher was the first on her long list of stops today. She would be spending the day 'getting the messages'. The woman smiled to herself as the phrase flitted through her mind. It took hearing her mother-in-law use the phrase several times before she finally figured out that it meant grocery shopping. Language and turns of phrase had always interested the woman, as though the secrets of a culture could be uncovered in the excavation of its colloquialisms and idioms. She'd once inquired about the origins of the phrase, but instead of the question generating further chat and connection, it was a conversation ender, so the next time she got curious she consulted the Internet for answers instead.

The woman only had a few hours before she had to get back to collect her daughters from daycare – 'crèche' it was called here – so she quickly made her way to the Luas. The tram would take her from the south Dublin suburb where they lived into the city centre where she would hopefully be able to tick off the rest of the items on her list.

That list was chock-full of ingredients from Puerto Rican cuisine: rice, pork, root vegetables and legumes. The Latino Caribbean culture of her father's family was not a mainstay on this island, but the woman was prepared to trawl through as many South Asian and African markets in the city centre as necessary to find exactly what she needed to make the slow-roasted pork, garlicky stewed rice and sticky sweet plantains, that, to her, were what Christmas tasted like.

The local butcher had been arguably the most important because if the *pernil* didn't turn out right, the meal would be incomplete. She'd consulted cookbooks and online recipes. She'd endured a lengthy FaceTime call with her father, who had told her everything *not* to do when prepping and cooking the pork shoulder. It'd be going into the oven before the kids even woke up on Christmas morning to cook all day, filling the house with aromas she could only describe to herself as the smells of Grandma's house.

It was a chilly but dry day, the sun doing its best to force its way for at least a few hours through the December clouds. She contemplated taking her sunglasses out of her bag, but as the Luas approached she thought better of it. Instead, she raised her face up to the weak rays and closed her eyes for just a moment. Her brown skin was at its palest at the moment – her 'winter shade', she called it – and even the slightest chance at natural vitamin D was enough to make her savour every moment her melanated skin could soak it in.

The Luas was busy for mid-morning on a Tuesday, but she anticipated that this close to Christmas. She finagled her way onto the first tram car, manoeuvring herself past ladies wielding collapsable shopping trolleys and an elderly gentleman with a walking stick. A teenager and her shopping bags took up a seat and a half, so the woman gestured to her, silently asking if she could place her bags on the floor. An eye roll and a sigh later, and the woman was settling into her window seat in front of a pair of older gentlemen engaged in conversation.

'Did you hear about your man?' one man was asking the other.

'Hah?' his companion shouted his reply.

'Your man, you know the one. The one in the estate, with the dog. Yeh, brown bread.'

'Feck off! Sure, I only saw him the other day.'

'There you are now.' The first man spoke with the authority of one who delivered such grave news regularly.

A heavy silence followed. The woman pulled her headphones over her ears.

It was two weeks until Christmas and she couldn't help but feel that she was leaving things a bit late this year. In typical fashion, she'd gotten all of the present buying out of the way by the first week of November – although she still found herself waking up in the middle of the night wondering if she'd gotten enough, or the same number of items, for each of her children.

But today wasn't about gifts. It was about food.

She'd had the thought to make a Puerto Rican Christmas dinner months ago when her Irish in-laws were over for her youngest daughter's birthday celebration. They were musing about the next time they would all be together, and how they couldn't wait for turkey and ham and all the many variations of potatoes that were a requirement of the annual feast.

While the woman understood the importance of traditions and respected those of her new home, she didn't share the nostalgic pull towards the dishes she had been served for the past three Christmases.

The Luas wound its way through the concrete neighbourhoods of Dublin and the woman let her mind wander back to the Christmases of her childhood. She remembered entering her grandparents' apartment, arriving in from a frigid New York evening, nose and toes numb from the cold, only to be met by the smells of her grandfather's cooking. The warmth of their home enveloped her instantly, and a hug from Grandma chased away the last remnants of the chill from outside, but it was the smells that told her she was home. The pungent, savoury smell of garlic was always the main feature, with the earthiness of oregano a close second, both necessary ingredients to create the succulent meats and rices that filled her family's table every year. Dessert was her grandmother's rice pudding, made with sweetened condensed milk and coconut. She remembered sucking the sweetness out of the spicy cinnamon tube she was lucky enough to uncover in her bowl one year as Grandma said, 'That means good luck for you in the new year, *mi nieta linda*,' before planting a kiss on her forehead.

Her mouth had begun to water at the memory and she mentally patted herself on the back for making the decision to bring her traditions to her new home this year.

Her Irish husband, who was more than happy to indulge in the food traditions of her ancestral home himself, had been concerned about the rest of his family, especially at such a sacred time. Ever since they had arrived three years ago – one child in tow already – to the joy of her in-laws who had welcomed their son and his family home with open arms, she'd been trying to find her footing, trying to find her place within their tight-knit family structure. There had been playdates with cousins, evenings of babysitting nieces and nephews, coffees with the sisters-in-law, but still, she couldn't help but feel like an outsider looking in when it came to family dynamics.

Food was the great unifier. Full bellies equal happy people. And she so very much wanted her family to be happy, and full.

The woman cued the video of a *pernil* recipe she found on Instagram on her phone, listening to the influencer's mix of rapid Spanish and English flow through her headphones as she described how to get the *chicharrón* to just the right level of crispiness.

She'd worked on translating the Spanish words for the ingredients she needed to find. She didn't speak Spanish, not fluently, but she knew the words for the ingredients to her favourite dishes. *Yuca*, *plátanos* and *gandules* – the pigeon peas would be the most difficult to find, but her father had promised to mail her some, along with some *sofrito*. She was worried that they wouldn't arrive in time so she was hoping to find close replacements today.

By the time she arrived at Abbey Street, the car she was on had gotten so full that she had to squeeze herself through to get to the doors. 'Sorry, sorry, sorry,' she said as she pushed past bags and shoulders. She'd removed her coat earlier in response to the oppressive warmth of the packed Luas, but she quickly zipped it up once more, bracing herself against the cold city air. The dynamic sounds of dozens of languages filled her ears and for just a moment, she felt like she was home in New York City. But then the Luas *dinged* to signal its departure and she was thrust back into the Dublin cityscape once more.

She headed to the South Asian shop on Parnell Street. Her friend from Venezuela had tipped her off that this was where she would find the most coveted of all the ingredients on her list: banana leaves. She absolutely needed these to make her grandma's signature dish, *pasteles*. The tiny parcels of plantain and meat, spiced with cumin and garlic, olives and capers, were what her parents had called 'an acquired taste' when she was little and had wrinkled her nose at the mushy substance wrapped in green leaves. But apparently puberty had provided her with the necessary tastebuds required to enjoy the most delicious part of Christmas by the time she turned twelve.

She made her way up O'Connell Street, a sudden wind threatening to send her back towards the Liffey. Her thoughts drifted back to watching her grandmother's brown hands as she cooked. Even though her grandfather had been a professional chef, only Grandma was allowed to make the *pasteles*. Her grandmother worked for days making the *masa* of plantains and pumpkin, grating the vegetables first before mashing them with a mortar and pestle and finally with her own hands. The woman pictured those hands working to form the small yellow parcels and wrap them in the green leaves that would impart their essence and help keep their shape as they boiled. Her grandmother would hum a tune the woman never got the chance to learn as she washed the dishes while the *pasteles* cooked.

Her grandmother was never far from her thoughts. She was a presence that the woman could feel looking over her shoulder, admiring the world right along with her. She found her often in the flavours of food, in her daughters' smiles, in the curve of her own hips.

Her body was complicated, her face full of brown freckles, wide nose and thick lips, atop a tall body full of curves. It made people wonder, made them question her origins. She understood, in a way. People need to be able to make sense of things around them, and mixed heritage was complicated for some to understand. As a result, she had spent forty years smoothing out her rough edges, shifting herself into something more palatable for others to digest. She'd attempted so many different things over the years, testing out different identities as someone else would try on clothes at the mall. But she was this *and* that, and that was complicated, nuanced, and difficult to understand, let alone explain. Even after all this time, after all this life she'd lived, she still found herself searching for a way to be that felt entirely her own.

But then there was food. Food had always been the easiest thing to use to illustrate her cultural mix. Her childhood friends may have been confused at her tenth birthday when they'd been served a meal of *Königsberger Klopse, spaetzle* and *flan* instead of pizza and birthday cake for her party. But her father had said she could have *anything* she wanted for her birthday, and the German meatballs and egg pasta and Puerto Rican creamy egg custard were her favourite foods, so he had begrudgingly obliged. Her father cooked everything from scratch (because that was the 'right way' to do things) and complained incessantly in the days leading up to her birthday about the time it would take to make it all. But he woke at dawn the morning of the day she turned ten and did it anyway. The smile on his face while she ate his food told her he probably didn't mind so much after all.

She loved the comforting German Jewish foods of her mother's family that filled her stomach like a warm blanket, but it was the Puerto Rican flavours of her father's side that spoke to her heart. She knew that the food of those ancestors had traversed continents and oceans. Generations ago, foreign ingredients had come together with indigenous food traditions to create something new and wonderful. And now she was bringing that food across an ocean, not to the place of its origin, but to a new place, where new traditions could be added to it and make something new again.

A man behind the till nodded to her and scents of cumin and cardamom warmed her nose as she walked down the narrow aisles. The tightness she didn't realise had been in her chest since the butcher's shop eased when her fingers wrapped around the hard cold package holding the dark-green leaves. She'd gotten the last bunch, she realised, releasing a breath.

The woman loaded up a basket with medium-grained rice and spices, and olives with pimentos and capers, and headed back to the till to pay. The shop owner, a middle-aged man with brown skin, smiled and nodded at her as she tapped her phone to pay. 'Happy Christmas,' he said with a Dublin lilt, as she loaded up her shopping bag and turned to leave.

She smiled back at him. 'Same to you.'

On the walk to Capel Street she passed mothers with small children in strollers laden with shopping bags that hung from their handlebars and were stuffed beyond the capacity of the storage space underneath. Notes of familiar Christmas tunes flitted out of open shop doors as she made her way to the Afro-Caribbean shop she was hoping would have *yuca* and *plátanos*.

Pausing outside the Brazilian hair salon, she looked through the large front windows of the Georgian building. She caught a glimpse of several tightly coiled heads bopping to the music she knew was most likely early 00s hip-hop and

R&B. The salon was typically buzzing with the soft staccato of Brazilian Portuguese, except for when the ladies belted out the English lyrics of a young Alicia Keys or Beyoncé. Their joy and laughter, and the fact that the stylists in there were among the first the woman had met in Dublin who actually understood how to cater to her multiracial hair, was why they had been her go-to salon for the past year and a half.

She paused on the sidewalk outside to check her calendar to make sure she had booked her appointment, but of course she had. She'd be back next Friday, two days before Christmas.

She checked the time. She'd have to hustle now to make it back home in time to pick up her girls. Actually, she needed to get back to the Luas at least fifteen minutes earlier than she'd planned because with her luck, the tram would be out of service or skipping stops and she'd have to scramble to find a bus that would get her back on time. Sweat was gathering in a pool on her back beneath her now too-warm winter coat and, as a cloud darkened the skies above, she realised that she'd made the rookie mistake of forgetting an umbrella.

The next shop had the starchy root vegetables and rich cooking bananas she'd been searching for. They even had cans of *gandules*, which meant her stewed rice would now be complete with all the textures and flavours that made it so perfect in her memory. She would let some of the *plátanos* ripen until they were mostly black – they would be at their sweetest when she peeled and cooked them slowly over a low flame, until the sugar within them crystallised into a slight crunch. Wishing she had more time to peruse the aisles bursting with wares that were foreign, yet somehow still familiar, the woman rushed to the till to pay.

Her arms weighed down with the full complement of ingredients on her list, the woman walked back out into the fading winter daylight. Despite her sense of urgency and the sweat gathering on her brow, her pace had slowed under the weight of all her 'bits'. A light rain began to fall as she made her way back towards Jervis Street to catch the Luas home.

The orange lettering of the electronic sign told her that the next tram was ten minutes away, if it was to be trusted, so she allowed her bags to rest on the ground. She would be cutting it close.

The woman put on her headphones and took out her phone. Engrossed in her search for a parenting podcast a friend had recommended, she jumped slightly at a soft tap on her shoulder.

She looked up to find a white man whose cheeks had turned rosy in the cold smiling at her. He had a Notre Dame knitted hat pulled over his grey hair and beside him was a woman she assumed was his wife. The wife had the distinct look of a person who has just eaten a sour cherry, her lips pressed together in such a tight line she almost looked like she didn't have any at all. Their attire and demeanour told her everything she needed to know about their country of origin before they opened their mouths to speak.

The woman gave them a small smile in return and pushed back her headphones, letting them hang around her neck.

'Does this Luas go to Dundrum?' The pinched tones of the man's rhotic Midwestern American accent grated on her ears. She hoped he didn't notice her wince.

'Ah, no,' she replied looking around briefly at the twenty-odd people waiting at the stop around them. Of all the people here, why had they chosen *her* to ask for directions? She had purposely brought her big bulky over-ear headphones for the commute as they were a clear indicator that she was not up for conversation. Wasn't it obvious that she wasn't from around here?

'Oh, right, OK. Honey – I told you we were in the wrong place.' He smiled at the woman again, almost apologetic for his partner's lack of civility.

'You're not far from where you need to be though,' the woman found herself explaining before they could turn away. She wondered if they could hear her own accent now above the din of the conversations and city noise around them. 'If you just keep walking that way,' she pointed to her right, 'you'll get to the Abbey Street stop. Keep going to the next intersection and you'll see the tracks for the Green Line on your left. That's the Luas you need.'

The American man's smile widened as he took in her directions, nodding along as she spoke. 'That's great. Thanks so much! Merry Christmas!' he said as he took his wife's hand and hurried them along. The wife's face relaxed, she seemed relieved to be leaving the immediate vicinity.

The car she was on took on elderly shoppers and young early holiday revellers in turn, no one spared the woman so much as a glance. By the time she got to her stop at the end of the line the sun had set. Christmas lights began to switch on one by one as she made her way through the familiar houses and apartment blocks of her neighbourhood. As she hurried past, the woman caught glimpses of families within the soft yellow glow of the homes around her: a baby giggling in a high-chair as its dishevelled father cleaned up an orange-coloured mess, siblings on a couch helping their parents unpack takeaway containers, a couple chatting while cooking dinner. The tableaus of home life made her smile but as the church bell tolled the hour she realised she was late for pickup.

As she walked into the créche, her arms and legs heavy with the burdens of her shopping, the worry and hurry of the day left her body as a softness overtook her. It was a softness she felt whenever she returned home after spending some time away.

'Mommy!' The voices of her daughters filled her heart as she dropped her shopping bags and gathered them in for a hug.

DECEMBER TWENTY-THIRD

Belinda McKeon

They both needed haircuts; their school uniforms were shrunken like anime costumes; they lived on plain pasta and Dr. Oetker Pizzinis; their fresh-air supply came mostly courtesy of the wind blowing open the front door of the Celtic Tiger semi-d on which we'd been almost impossibly lucky to get a six-month lease; the seven-year-old was having toddler tantrums again, the five-year-old was love bombing everyone he met with the precision and cunning of a cult leader, and the safety filters on YouTube Kids, I had finally noticed, were about as effective as the face yoga to which I subjected myself to every night before bed.

But, back in August, when our return to Ireland had still felt like a novelty, not to mention a good idea, I had secured premium-slot tickets for the *Winter Forestland Experience*, the kind of premium-slot tickets of which only a pristinely organised, combatively focused mother could boast: so how bad could things be? It was December twenty-third, sunset was slated for nine minutes past four, and we were going to a Forest Thing, with the children dressed in the navy- and-red Bonpoint and Petit Bateau separates I'd gathered over the past couple of weeks – OK, months – and tracked on a spreadsheet entitled *Lookbook Kids Xmas 25*. There'd be the cosy air pollution of fairy lights, tens of thousands of them draped and twinkling along walkways crunching with confused autumnal leaf-fall; there'd be NCAD students dressed as elves; there'd be hot chocolate in ceramic mugs, not polyurethane cups, there'd be educational wooden presents from Santa. The children would despise the presents and wail about the surface temperature of the ceramic mugs, and Christ knew what they'd deliver in response to the Gen Z elven stares, but I'd feel like I'd done something right, after months of getting everything wrong.

I'd have something for the grid. I'd lob a miniature Baileys into my ceramic mug. Josh would be driving; I could sleep in sweet oblivion, afterwards, all the way home.

Or so I thought, until I remembered the Lily Thing.

The Lily Thing and the Forest Thing, it turned out, had been scheduled for the same time, but they could not take place at the same time, because they each required me, and the children – and yes, probably Josh, if only as the driver.

Josh, I had by this point in my re-emigration odyssey accepted, would not be partaking in any real way in anything this Christmas. Josh was out of it: likely anhedonic, ChatGPT had surmised. The move back here, I kept reminding myself – and silently reminding Josh – had been Josh's idea. It had been possible because of the competitive global footprint of Josh's parent company. It had been expedient because of the descent into competitive authoritarianism of Josh's parent country. It had been abhorrent to Josh's actual parents, who considered their son and grandchildren part of the amenities package of their life as retirees in Northern New Jersey, but: oh, well. It had made sense for us to get out. We had been fortunate to get out. Yes, Josh missed his family, and his culture, and his friend group, and his Mets, and OK yes, he missed his three-bedroom duplex in Crown Heights, but did he think I did not miss that same three-bedroom duplex – *our* three-bedroom duplex – in Crown Heights?

Because yes, I missed it. There were days when I missed the roaches. There were days when I even missed the landlord. But needs must. Our children had learned how to hide from gunfire before they had learned to write their names. Life in the old country might be colourless, it might be predictable, but how much vibrancy and adventure does a person need?

To wit: the Lily Thing.

Lily was my maiden aunt, the depressive eldest sister of my depressive elderly father, who had spent her entire working life as the housekeeper to the parish priest of a large suburban sprawl in southside Dublin. When that charismatic padre – by then canon – had breathed his last, she had taken to her bed, and shortly afterward to the County Kildare nursing home, for the care of which she was not, at that stage, yet a truly needful candidate, but into the nonenal-scented maze of which, nevertheless, she insisted upon propelling herself at the age of seventy-four. I remembered her grand relocation there because it had taken place the summer I had relocated myself, and before leaving for New York I had visited Lily in Pine Brooks, bringing flowers, drinking MiWadi, coming away with a guilt migraine and a renewed determination to get on the other side of Customs and Border Protection at JFK.

Now, though, I was back, and now Lily was ninety, and for the first time in many years – the first time, certainly, since the children were born – I could be a part of the festive family tradition known as the Lily Thing, or The Thing for Lily, in which everyone – my parents, my siblings and their families, my other living aunts and uncles and their available offspring and accessories – gathered, with bright faces and baked goods and beribboned parcels, around Lily in her bed in her nursing home, and made cheerful noises and pulled vexating crackers, and took photos and video for WhatsApp family group evidence, before evacuating as a unit and as an energy field until December twenty-third of the following year.

Was it fair? Would individual visits, perhaps even more frequent individual visits, have been more thoughtful, more generous, more considerate of poor Lily's situation, her central nervous system, her deep and caustic hatred for all things cheerful, and festive, and beribboned?

But it was Christmas, and nobody had time to cogitate over such things. As for me, I had been absent from those Lily Thing WhatsApps for long enough – or rather, my beautiful, Bonpointed children had been absent for long enough. This December twenty-third would see us installed in our rightful place around the medical bed and its siderail controls. Lily had never even met my children! Lily, who had prayed that I might conceive them (I had not asked for such prayers; my mother had informed me, on both occasions, that they had been successful, and that a card to Lily would be in order); Lily, for whom (if one ignored the existence of Josh's mother, Lillith), our daughter might be argued to have been given her second name.

The Lily Thing was at 3pm, and the Winter Forestland booking was for an hour later. The Winter Forestland was an hour away from the nursing home. If we reached the nursing home exactly at the appointed time, I reasoned, and stayed for twenty minutes (just long enough for photographs, some light ribbon-ripping, and a chorus of 'Stop the World and Let Me Off', or whatever it was my family were always singing to Lily in the Lily Thing videos), we'd make it to the Winter Forestland just twenty minutes late, which would still leave time to move through all the Elf Stages, albeit a little more rapidly than recommended, toward the hot chocolate and twinkly eyed Santa and undyed pine Jenga sets and abacuses (*What the fuck am I supposed to do with an abacus*, I imagined my daughter raging), and I would get the photographs taken, and get the core memories made, and I would have the miniature Baileys, maybe two (maybe three), and Christmas would be … what was the term?

Unlocked.

'We can do this,' I said to Josh, on the morning of the twenty-third. 'We can make this work.'

Josh looked up from his phone, and I could see in the hollowness of his gaze just how long it had been since his American prescription had run out, and just how long we had left to find an Irish GP who was accepting new patients, and who would prescribe Josh the same SSRI, before – before what?

I had discovered immense benefit from the practice of no longer finishing my thoughts, of no longer allowing myself to articulate my own questions. It was, I had decided, a new kind of mindfulness. You cannot spiral, cannot catastrophise, if you interrupt yourself before the first deft curve of the spiral, the first rich layer of the catastrophe, has had a chance to take hold in your thinking.

Having come to the end of my own SSRI prescription, it might be mentioned, I was microdosing psilocybin truffles imported from a supplier in Rotterdam and paid for in Bitcoin. That might have been helping things, or worsening them; like I say, I didn't finish the thoughts. I just pushed onward. If an Instagram algorithm caught me at exactly the right moment, as had been the case with the lavish pitch deck for the *Winter Forestland Experience*, I was capable of great things, great and all-encompassing intentions. I could buy Pilates rings, retinol creams, vitamin gummies, parenting courses; I could download walking coaches, ADHD regulators, alcohol trackers, finance podcasts. I could *add to cart* my future, my children's futures; I could build capsules, wishlists, snag lists, gratitude lists.

In truth, since we had moved home, the family WhatsApp chats had been underwhelming: much sparser, less connected, more meme-laden than I had, in my emigrant wistfulness, imagined; as for the actual family meetings, the in-person heart-to-hearts and the quality time that only proximity and familiarity could facilitate: well, whoop, there goes the spiral again, before I've even grabbed a hold of the curve. Had this been a mistake? Friendships, community, the duplex on Park Place, right by the Children's Museum – but think of the chill that seized down the whole body every time a siren sounded out on the street, heading down towards the schoolyard, every day there was school. And now: think of the snatchings. Agents. Masked mouths. A well-regulated militia, with unregulated blood sugar.

So. We bloom where we're planted. We look forwards, not backwards. We find a doctor. We find a dentist. We get a 4.5 per-cent interest rate on a mortgage to bring us into our nursing-home years. We count our blessings, and the rest, we leave to the algorithm. Make the lists. Chase the truffles. *Impossibly lucky*: remember that phrase.

'Did you say something?'

I stared at Josh, or at Josh's stare.

'Did I say something?' I replied.

He shook his head.

Then he saw the children, in the outfits in which I'd put them for the day. He stared: a different kind of stare.

'It's just for the photographs,' I said, as I got our daughter into her velvet-trimmed coat.

The old Josh would have said something like, *Who's taking them, Sir Cecil Beaton?* But this Josh, the Josh who couldn't tear himself away from *POLITICO* or *The Hill*, from the X feed – from the videos, from the messages from his brothers, from his college friends: this Josh just shrugged.

And at the nursing home, this Josh said he would stay in the car. The children asked to do the same, but I made them come with me. A nurse buzzed us in, and as we followed her through the corridors, I played the mental game I always played, walking through a space that had been decorated and furnished as though it had been a home. I imagined versions of the moment in which each piece of decor had been purchased: this framed picture, this armchair, this vase, this occasional table, this frilled curtain. Someone had chosen each of these things, picked them off a shop floor or from a catalogue, and had thought, what? *That's lovely?* Had thought, *That'll be nice in the Alzheimer's hallway?* Or, had they thought, *That'll do, that's cheap, who gives a fuck what we lob into that place? A framed print of a horse cart, no horse, but beside the wheels, a tongue-lolling golden retriever? Grand. These half-naked cherubs? Grand. Nobody's going to be looking that closely. Nobody's going to be passing down this corridor thinking about how these pieces are in conversation.*

The nurse's face had softened when I had told her we had come to see Lily. It was good we were here, she'd told us. Lily was in her room.

Were we the first, I had asked, but the nurse had not replied, and my daughter had been demanding to know who Lily was, and my son had been trying to open the lid of the grand piano in the foyer. I was nervous, I realised: it was several years since I had seen my aunt, and while the children would provide plenty of material for small talk, still I was not sure what to say to her. How to greet her.

When I was a teenager, I had visited her by myself, for two or three days of a summer holiday, in the presbytery where she lived, not with the priest but downstairs from him, in a self-contained flat. She had an electric fireplace with fake coal, and a television with the English stations, and a backyard that was oddly curtailed, hemmed in by a high breeze-block wall, as though it had once been a proper back garden, but had then been sliced and narrowed to a strip just wide and long enough for a clothes line and the clatter of bins.

Which, as it turned out, was exactly what had happened, except that the garden had, before being sliced and narrowed into this cement alleyway, been not just a garden but a swimming pool.

'Filled in now,' Lily had told me, in the next moment. 'Father Fox had to get it filled in again.'

'Why?' I whined, crestfallen. It was just my luck. A pool before I came here, and now no pool, because the priest had decided to do away with it? I hated him, I decided. I hated his pool-filling ways, and his footstep in the large, austere house above us, his dark dining room with its paintings of saints, its sideboards of whiskey and brandy in cut crystal, its commemorative clocks.

'Not fair,' I said.

'Believe me, you wouldn't want to go in,' Lily replied crisply. 'Nothing but mischief happened in there. That was the last priest, of course. Not Father Fox.'

Mischief sounded good. The last priest sounded more fun than this one. Why couldn't I have visited her during the last priest's time?

'He only let boys in there anyway, love,' she told me. 'Even if it was still there now, you wouldn't be let in.'

My aunt in those days was a short, stout woman with a tight perm and a strict routine. She made the priest's breakfast, she went to Mass, she did the shopping, she cooked the lunch, then the dinner, she did the laundry, and she watched the evening news. Only her laugh was surprising; it was a loud laugh, whooping and delighted, and when she laughed, it always sounded as though something unreasonable had been unmoored. It made her sound manic, which was not something that could be said of any other aspect of the way my aunt lived; nothing else about her was anything but orderly, and nothing else about her was delighted, nothing at all. When my aunt Lily laughed, people stared. It sounded less like laughter than like unconsolable sobbing.

'Here we are,' said the nurse now, with a smile.

She pushed the door open. The room was in semi-darkness, and I could make out only the shapes of its contents: a wardrobe, a side table with framed photographs and prayer cards, a television, which was not on. An LED candle flickered on the windowsill. In the hospital bed was a tiny person: she looked like a child of nine or ten. Her hair was a soft, blurred wisp; her cheekbones were like hinges in her skin. Her eyes were sunken, and there was no question of a conversation with her. There was no question of small talk.

'Is that lady dead?' my daughter demanded.

'No, she is not dead,' the nurse said firmly. 'She is comfortable.'

I wanted to move closer, to understand more completely, but I found myself unable to take a step forwards or backwards. It had been a long time, and my family had told me that Lily was declining, but as I searched her face for traces of the person I had known, what I thought I could glimpse was not the woman in that house in Dublin, or the woman who had come to my childhood home for occasional three-day holidays of her own, but the women who had come before her: the ancestors, my ancestors, known only to me from tattered and tiny sepia photographs. She was her own grandmother now, maybe, her grandmother's grandmother, or grandfather, even. She was Victorian; Norman; medieval.

'Hello, Lily,' I said, looking down at her.

'It won't be long now,' the nurse said kindly.

My head shot up.

'I'm sorry?'

The nurse reinforced her sympathetic smile. 'The doctor was in with her this morning. He said a matter of hours.'

'Hours?' I repeated weakly. 'To die?'

'DIE?' my daughter howled, and I tried in vain to shush her, while her brother started up howling too.

'Her heart rate has slowed,' the nurse enunciated over the racket. 'Her breathing as well. I'll leave you alone for a while?'

'But I don't understand,' I said, as she moved for the door. 'Are we the first?'

She stopped. 'The first?' she said gently. 'You think others are coming?'

'Oh, they're definitely coming,' I said.

'I see,' she said lightly, and she left.

I stared at my aunt in the over-engineered contraption that was her bed. Castors, levers, panels: was this what it took to die? And since when had she been dying, anyway? Did anyone else in the family know? Such a cavalier attitude to death should not have surprised me in a nursing home, I supposed, but still. Or did they know, and had just not bothered to tell me? Was the WhatsApp inertia really so extreme?

I looked at my two small children in their Christmas coats, hovering near the foot of their great-aunt's deathbed, their faces uncertain, lollipops from the front desk clutched, unopened, in their hands.

'Come here,' I beckoned them. 'I need to explain something to you.'

'What?' they frowned in unison.

'This is my auntie,' I said, gathering them to me.

'We know that,' my daughter said.

'Right, and she's very old. You see?' I indicated the bony face, the darkened eye sockets, the shrivelled skin of her hands on the blanket, already wrapped in their rosary beads.

'Why does she have her necklace on her fingers like that?' my daughter asked.

'Is she going to die?' said my son.

'Yes,' I said, firmly, and I brought them closer to me. 'She is going to die.'

'Now?' my daughter said in a shocked voice, pulling away.

'Not *right* now, but very soon. We're just,' I said, swallowing, 'I suppose we're just here to say goodbye to her.'

'OK,' my daughter said, in Lily's direction. 'Goodbye.' Then she turned to me. 'Can we go now? I want to open that piano.'

'Goodbye,' her brother said, heading for the door.

'Wait!' I said. 'I have to stay for a while. Until the others get here.'

As the whining started up, I said, 'I'll let you watch YouTube on my phone.'

'OK,' my son said instantly, springing towards it, but I held it away from him: I needed to shoot a text to Josh.

Different situation here than I thought, I typed. *Come in? Need you to take kids.*

'OK, Lily,' I said a moment later, phone handed off, MrBeast giving a tour of LA real estate to my children in the corner. 'I'm here, love,' I said, and I pulled a chair up to her bedside.

Some time later, I was still there, and the kids were complaining that they were hungry, and that the battery warning had come up on the phone screen. Lily was still breathing. Josh hadn't turned up. My family hadn't turned up. It seemed to be getting dark outside, but I had no idea what time it was, and I was running out of Lily memories to scroll through in my mind as I made the effort to hold her in my heart in gratitude, etc.

'Give me the phone,' I said, and from the corner came a wail of protest.

'Just for a second,' I said. 'I need to call Dad.'

When I took it, the screen was gridlocked with notifications.

'Why didn't you tell me I had messages?' I asked the kids, pointlessly.

Where are you

We're here

Hello????

I didn't bother trawling through the rest of them. I called my sister. She picked up immediately.

'Where the fuck are you?'

I could barely speak with astonishment. 'I'm with *Lily*,' I said slowly. 'Where do you think I am?'

'What?'

'Where are *you*, is the question. Where are all of you?'

My sister paused a moment before answering. '*We* are with Lily.'

The room seemed to arch and blur for a moment. I looked at my screen again. Josh had texted me. *FFS Grace where u at?*

'You can't be with Lily,' I told my sister. 'I am with Lily. I'm keeping vigil—'

'Hang on a minute,' my sister said, and I thought I could hear a quiver in her voice; was she crying? Then, her voice away from the phone a little, she said, 'She's keeping vigil beside someone she thinks is Lily.'

'Ah for fuck's sake!' I heard, and that was my mother's voice, and there was my father's, saying precisely the same thing, and there was a whoop of laughter – I knew that laughter – that laughter belonged to Josh.

Well. At least that was something.

'Grace,' my sister said into the phone now. 'I don't know whose bedside you're at, or who you've kept vigil for. Her name may well be Lily. But she's not *our* Lily. Our Lily is in the TV room, with her friends, and we got tired of waiting for you to arrive, so we did the presents.'

'You did the presents?' I said numbly. 'And the photos?'

'And your husband is here,' my sister said, more quietly now. 'What's wrong with him?'

'What do you mean, what's wrong with him?' I said. 'Can he hear you?'

'No,' my sister said, 'I've stepped out of the room. Seriously, what's the story with him? There are oul' fellas in here who look brighter than him.'

'He's depressed,' I said.

'We're all depressed,' my sister said dismissively. 'Get over it.'

'Yeah,' I said.

'So are you coming over to join us?' My sister said. 'Or are you going to wait until the other Lily dies?'

'Mom!' my daughter shouted, banging her little fists against the side table laden, I saw now, with photographs of strangers. 'We need the phone!'

'And I think your auntie is dead,' said my son, pointing at the woman in the bed. She was not, but that couldn't be helped. 'Come on,' I said. 'Let's go see Santa.'

'*Santa* is in here?' my daughter said in horror.

We were late for the Winter Forestland, and the tickets were not valid for any slot other than the slot for which we'd paid. I argued my case at the desk, that a relative had been dying in a nursing home, that there had been a family emergency, but they wouldn't listen. The children sobbed, and then someone behind the desk took pity on them randomly and said we could go in, but we'd have to move quickly through the experiences in order to get to Santa's hut within the appropriate timeframe. You have five experiences to get through, she explained, showing me the map. Each of them has a challenge. Each challenge takes between five and ten minutes, usually, but given that it's forty-five minutes past the hour now, you'll need to complete each challenge within—

'Ten minutes,' Josh interjected, helpfully. He'd gotten out of the car, to my amazement.

'Two minutes per challenge,' the attendant said. 'Do you think you can do that?'

At the fifth and final challenge, which was something to do with Mrs Claus – a woman my own age sat in a staged sitting room with a blanket over her legs and an electric fireplace glowing beside her. The children were hopped up on the adrenaline of it all, and I was limping from having tripped over a tree branch a few challenges ago. But the kids were racing ahead. They were soft-haired and ridiculously dressed and full of hope and consumerism and belief, and as we watched them hurtle towards Mrs Claus, a helpful elf urging them along, with Mrs Claus taking a moment to hide her vape under the blanket on her lap, Josh, beside me, took my hand.

'There they go,' he said.

I leaned my head on his shoulder.

In Mrs Claus's enclosure, a fake fire burned, and the fake tree was hung with little fake candles.

'Wherever they're going,' I said.

And I closed my eyes.

SWANS

Tim MacGabhann

Milena knew it was bougie to get catering in, but without Leilani from Brasília going around with the sambo squares on the blue plate and checking the drinks levels she'd be literally run off her feet.

Just being on coat duty had her up to ninety as it was: a drift heaped on the queen-size in the second bedroom, beige trench, kiddos' puffas, a camel greatcoat, school-shootery leathers, belonging to Brendan and Tess, to her and her husband Freddi and to their kiddos Kostas and Eva, as well as to Willow, to Leilani, to Tess's kid, Arden – and Fionn and Louise yet to arrive. God, a bed filled up so fast didn't it? A cold winter smell breathed up from the heap: leather, wool, trapped atoms of chimney smoke from outside. Hardly had she let fall Willow's belted thigh-length number in olive wool than the door buzzer shrilled again and she'd to go out to receive more. Shaking her head, Milena went via the hall through the hubbub overflowing from the kitchen already.

'Oh, I'm *obsessed* with her,' she heard Tess say. 'She's so cool. She has such a fashionable drug habit.'

Milena unstuck a sweaty lock of hair from her forehead, then pasted herself against the wall to let Eva and Kostas charge past her – Kostas shrieking, Eva's pigtails whapping her thigh. She took a second to breathe and to push down the question as to why she put this night on. But she always did it: had done, every year, in the last weekend before Christmas, since they'd all left college. This was the fifteenth instalment. Around the core of Tess, Willow, Milena, and Louise – they'd shared the same scholarship flat on campus – numbers had shrunk and dilated not just around the births of Kostas, Eva and Arden, but around other comings and goings too: the sudden, crunchy ending of Tess's marriage; Milena's stint in Berlin, from which she'd returned with the acclaimed local sculptor Freddi in tow; Willow's disappearance into Nicaragua, from which she'd returned as a poet, midwife and addiction doula. Of the men, only Fionn was a true mainstay. Brendan, who was a whole nine years younger than Tess, had come along after her separation. He was OK, Brendan, but always turned up at these things with a bag, let things get out of hand.

Although why complain about small stuff, Milena thought, primping the coat heap so nothing would get too wrinkled. She'd been stressed out about people arriving too late, and now she was stressed about them arriving at bang on seven, as if in a relay. She needed to just chill. She put her hand on the doorlock. Through the spyhole, heads bulged and swimmy, stood Fionn and Louise. She shut her eyes, gave in to the headachey press of the air in the hallway. From the kitchen came the zippy aquatic bass line and just-come-up heartbeat urgency of hi-hats: a playlist she'd put on to maybe shuffle back college for all of them – the good bits, not the ratty pills and the too-loud laughter in dorm corridors, not the shags with at best only semi-embarrassing types where you felt like the whole world was listening to you through the wall. But the hopeful uplift in the chord progression – so managed, so tinny – brought back nothing only panic, aimed, as it was, towards somewhere in her chest that either no longer existed or else never had. The thought made her aware that even the backs of her upper arms felt slick with coolish sweat.

Kostas roared. Eva giggle-squealed. Back they charged the way they'd come, into the glow of the kitchen.

'Buzzer not working?' Milena heard Louise mutter through the door, and Fionn tried it again, sending a wire of pain and tension humming right through the core of her skull. She blew out a sigh that flapped her lips and opened the door to the last of the guests.

Fionn stood in front of the door smoothing fluff from his wool blazer. His hands were right over his nipples when Milena swung the door open.

'Hi-ii,' she said, in a panicked trill, her eyes goggling: a horse who's realised at one and the same time both that it must bolt, and cannot.

'Oh my God you look fit to drop,' said Louise. 'Are you alright?'

'Yeah, can we help you with anything?' said Fionn.

'No no no, you're grand,' said Milena, waggling her hands. She brushed back her fringe.

‘We brought bits,’ said Louise, and Fionn lifted from the floor a paper bag that contained one Tupperware of aubergine and mushroom shawarma, with another of roasted cauliflower. The whole evening had gone low sugar and alcohol free, as well as veggie, because that suited most lists.

‘Heroic,’ said Milena, and took the bag from him.

Fionn let Louise in first, then followed – but too abruptly, nearly clumping into a young woman holding a blue plate.

‘Sambo square?’ she said, proffering the plate. *She was hot*. Fionn couldn’t help thinking that complete sentence.

‘I thought you’d never get here,’ said Milena.

‘It’s all on me,’ said Louise, shaking her head. ‘Everything takes me so long. Fionn just showers and throws on a shirt. Or is that internalised sexism?’

‘I try to put in a bit more effort than that,’ said Fionn. He was wiggling his feet from his Chelsea boots.

Milena, a hand to her forehead, said, ‘Oh, Jesus, do I smell smoke?’

Louise squeezed Fionn’s forearm and grimaced.

‘Yeah, go cool her down,’ he said. ‘I’ll be there in a tick.’

‘Thanks, babes,’ she said, and followed Milena up the hall, leaving Fionn standing there with the woman holding both the blue plate and Louise’s coat.

‘Give us that,’ he said to her. ‘You’re laden.’

‘That’s very nice of you,’ she said, and beamed, and handed him the plate. Part of him melted the way it did just before kick-off in five-a-side.

He went into the second bedroom, as discs of condensation cleared from his glasses lenses, then turned to take Louise’s coat from Leilani.

'Rotten out there.' He felt a queasy mix of sweaty from the rush and wet from the sleet. These sweats made him feel how little good the running and the kettlebells were doing him, aesthetically speaking. He still flushed patchily, across the cheeks and the temples, and whatever apparent runner's high you were supposed to get never felt memorable enough to become a true motivation. In fact, it just made him feel as though his whole world had become the experience of being on a run: that feeling of being always slightly behind, slightly too slow, and seeping sweat from bits of your body that you didn't often remember existed. As he doffed his wool blazer he flapped the back of it in two ventilating wings that only pasted the pineapple shirt he'd on even more tightly to his back.

'Although,' he added, and pushed up his glasses, 'the right side of the house is out, as my granny used to say.'

The woman with the plate laughed tonelessly, but then had mercy on him, adding, 'You know nothing about rain in Ireland.'

'Oh yeah?' he said, drawing together the shoulders of his coat so it hung limp across her hand. 'What's it like where you're from?'

'Brasília,' she said. 'The clouds look like bombers.'

'I'd say it's mad there,' he said. 'You a friend of Milena's, is it?'

'I'm just helping,' she said. 'For the evening. I'm Leilani.' She put out a hand that felt coolly slick with what he assumed – by the scent around her – was cocoa butter.

'Fionn,' he said, and sniffed. 'Oh. I think that is actual smoke actually.'

'Oh,' said Leilani. 'Yeah. Me too. I'll be right back.'

Fionn realised he'd left his phone in his blazer, then went rooting in the heap for it. Which pocket was it even in?

'Oho, there he is!' said a male voice from the doorway.

Fionn turned, one forearm lodged up the satiny sleeve lining of his blazer, to see Brendan, who – apart from the undercut and floppy fringe, which was a bit polyamory coded – was probably the person most similar to him at these pre-Chrimbo things: a full-stack developer from Coolock; a boy done good; a United fan; and the owner of a discreet, cuboid weed vape, which he was now sucking on.

Brendan was the newest addition to things, even though he wasn't that new. It'd been about eighteen months. Tess had been on a plane sitting beside him flying back from Art Basel to Dublin. He'd been over for some computery conferencey thing. Things had been bad between Tess and her then-husband, Jan. Tess and Brendan had kissed – not even had sex, just kissed – on the flight. Fionn wouldn't think much of himself if he cheated on Louise, but there had to have been force-majeure shit going on for Tess to spend the first twelve hours away from Jan in maybe years getting tipsy in first class and shifting the lad beside her. Nobody'd really blamed her: they'd blamed Jan. Sometimes cheating was alright. What do you do to a wife to make her think she has to do that the second she's out of sight? What kind of entrapped, stuck-champagne-cork type frustration must she be in?

And then, after she'd told him, he'd flipped out. She'd fled the gaff while it was still dark, and she'd wound up Coke-canned from behind by a van. They kept her in for two days, released her once she was out of the concussion woods, and she'd moved into her studio. The last Fionn had seen of Jan was when he'd handed him a Puma go-bag of Tess's things one morning. He'd never known Jan well. He'd been achingly polite the whole time, to the point where Fionn had felt like he might blow. Since the things handover, his last impression of Jan had begun to blur. As he'd foisted a neatly parcelled chunk of his wife's life across the doormat to him, Jan's lid became a hammered thumb, an eggish hectic promontory that poked up, half-bearded, from the tight neck of his polo. His head was a rage erection, thrust up to the world as though to say, *Look how much you hurt me you fuck! You owe me relief!*

But the weirded-out anger Fionn felt at the state of him was less immediate repulsion in that moment than a retrospective add-on, because he'd never *dis*liked him. He'd just never gotten them as a couple. Jan inhibited her. There was nothing they did together that she couldn't have done alone, career-wise, and yet she was so keen always to do the admin side of their architectural firm, while he did the vision bit. Her own vision bit would have been more than sufficient – and so it had proved, more or less, in the year and a half since.

Brendan jetted a pale vapeguest from the corner of his mouth, then croaked, 'Want a bang of the happy box?' He held the discreet black cuboid out to Fionn.

'The social-adeptness box,' said Fionn, pulling his arm from the sleeve and making grateful prayer hands at Brendan. The phone could wait. He didn't want to be seen scrolling anyway. 'You utter king.'

'Alhamdulillah,' said Brendan, as the motor inside the vape whinnied and Fionn sucked down a jungly scud. 'A bunch of coffee-roaster lads grow it in a polytunnel in Thomastown. Beside a paddy field.'

'Side hustle,' said Fionn tightly.

'Yeah, dawg,' said Brendan, and sat down on the edge of the bed. 'Pit stop.'

'Kiddo tiring, is it?' asked Fionn.

'Ah, no,' said Brendan. 'They're at school and that. Between that and all the parties I barely see them. I'm just a crock.' He lifted the cloth of his skinny black jeans to resettle the fabric. 'School's going grand though. Arden fancies their teacher but they're only eight so I can't see it going anywhere.'

''Tis tough,' said Fionn, and let himself sink down beside Brendan, hands in his pockets, thumbs out. Another plume hissed from his mouth, cooling his lips. 'So she's "they" now is she? They.'

'That's right, yeh,' said Brendan. Arden wasn't his kid: they belonged to Jan, Tess's ex. He'd stepped in pretty smoothly, all things considered, even if Arden had taken a while to thaw out.

'And you were alright with that or …' said Fionn.

'Sure, what else would I be?' said Brendan.

'I didn't mean your opinion, just …'

'Oh yeah, no, obviously,' said Brendan. 'What other kids say and shit.'

'Teachers, even.'

'Yeah, but it's not as hard a road as it used to be. Youse were never tempted, or …' said Brendan, and stopped himself. 'Like in terms of kids. Or. Is that insensitive?'

Fionn flapped a hand and said, 'Not in the least, no, we'd zero real desire.' Even mentioning the pre-snip days gave him the queasy fear he'd get when Louise was late – a worry, primarily, for their finances; secondarily, for the ecological impact of a developed-world kiddo knocking around; and, tertiarily, for the holiday-budget-slash-time aspect, as they tried to see as much of the world before it melted or flights were curtailed by government controls or whatever.

'Fair play,' said Brendan. 'And the writing?'

Fionn shrugged, said, 'Just reviews. It's OK.'

After college, Fionn had tried to get a Film Studies PhD off the ground: imperialism in modern American cinema – *too diffuse*, allegedly, even though if he'd pitched it in any of the last nine years since he'd have been in, no bother.

'Scratches the itch, does it?' said Brendan, with a twitch of the shoulder.

'I can do it on the side, even in work time,' said Fionn. He now worked in mental-health service provision, civil service side. This was a lateral switch out of asylum-seeker and refugee care. He'd had to get out. This time last year he'd been battling to get a broken heater fixed in a marquee on the grounds of a primary school. This marquee had only been erected because the hotel where the people were usually sheltered hadn't wanted to miss out on the festive bookings. He'd gone down to the marquee himself. Even with the rad mended, the heat had begun at his knees. Everything below was wettish ice: everything above a throat-drying parch – Hell, really, you'd have to say. Where all those people were tonight, he'd no idea.

On the way in, a spattery wind had rattled the taxi windows. In the doorway of 'The Dead' house on Usher's Island they'd put in homeless spikes ahead of the renovation. Only a couple of weeks before, cycling past on one of the bright days, there'd been a huddle of bags and a few fellas in beanie hats standing around. He'd thought the word *Dickensian*. What adjective belonged to the metal portcullis laid across the doorway in their place, he couldn't think.

'Nice, bro,' said Brendan, nodding, as Fionn had a third – or was it fourth? – huff on the vape.

'And the computers?' Fionn passed across the vape.

'The computers,' Brendan laughed.

'I'm sorry,' said Fionn. 'I don't know enough to be more specific.'

'You haven't to be,' said Brendan, taking back the vape for another go. 'They're grand. They're killing us. But they are also grand about it.' He double tapped the button on the happy box and said, 'That'll do me unless you want more?'

Fionn waved his hands.

'I don't touch the sauce anymore, you see,' said Brendan. 'Marijuana maintenance programme. It's permitted. Ish.' He shook the box. 'Grey area stuff.'

'Usually I just do bag,' said Fionn. 'Or pints. But this was alright.'

'Yeah, it's a gentle blend,' said Brendan. 'Widow or haze makes me feel like I'm trapped in an underground car park. Or a Massive Attack album.'

'Which one?'

'*Mezzanine*.'

'Fuck.'

Brendan uttered a dirty chuckle and gave a sideward nod at the door, then said, 'We should knock in. Now we're adept.' He pushed himself up from the bed with his fists, then pulled with him Fionn, who was slower to get upright.

In the steamy fug of the kitchen they'd put two square tables end to end. The smoke issue now sorted, Tess and Louise were neatening the cloth, while Leilani stood to one side, holding a tray that bore two large clay bowls. On the sideboard were arrayed vegan sashimi bites, tuna-dark tongues of soy or seitan or something. Riskily, they'd chosen the top of the weighted-key piano as a sideboard for the drinks and desserts. Brendan, feeling it less than Fionn, slunk in beside Tess to help. She withdrew her head from him and gave him a look of playful suspicion, to which he answered, 'Guilty … as charged.'

'Get the pots from Leilani, will you,' she said. Tess was chill too, in fairness. She taught English in Loreto Dalkey, and expressed, often, a particular warmth for goths and emos, because there were so few kids who weren't white there, and she had to take what riot of difference amid the bleached whiteness and eating disorders that she could get.

Fionn hung on just inside the door, that pocket of cool within the room's headache warmth, and watched Milena's partner, Freddi, walk towards him with the mock-slow steps of a bear, saying, 'Well, well, well, if it isn't the big man!' then added, 'Literally,' because Fionn was six-five, and Freddi was not.

'Oh, very good,' said Fionn. 'How's things?'

'I'm so well,' said Freddi, shaking his head, as though amazed by his own well-being. 'So, so well.' A little older than fifty, Freddi wore a steel-grey baker-boy cap at a jaunty angle over a head shaven to conceal baldness. His stubble shone like mica on his jaw. He, like Milena, with her owlish hauteur, was hot. Fionn wanted the happy box again very badly.

While Freddi asked Brendan questions about his year, Fionn let himself drift internally, scan the room. Freddi and Milena's new apartment was big, a duplex, but oddly shaped: the bedrooms and bathrooms were entered into downstairs via a curtain, as though heading underground. But a security light poured through the skylights, and the back window over the media room gave onto the water feature of the complex – a not-inspiring one, Fionn conceded, watching the lopped pizzle of the fountain leak brown water into browner.

'Hi, you!' said Willow, approaching in a waft of lilacky perfume, arms flung wide, pulling Fionn into a one-armed hug. In the other hand she held a tawny pitcher of kombucha, which did not slosh. 'Long time.' She fetched a glass and glugged it full for him.

'Has been, yeah, you good?' he said.

'Oh, sublime, yeh, I am loving this kombucha Freddi made,' said Willow, and clinked her glass against his.

'For my IBS,' said Freddi. 'It's incipient.'

'Anxiety causes it,' said Willow.

'And meat,' said Brendan, at whose behest the whole thing was meat free. This meant that Freddi's brisket expertise would go unasked for, although he now began to talk about it all the same, describing what the others were missing, to mute nods meant neither to encourage nor abash. A chunk of ginger bumped Fionn's lip as he nodded, drank.

'Got a kick to it,' he said, he thought to no one, but Willow gave a low disdainful laugh.

'Said every white person ever,' she said, lowering the pitcher to the table. 'At Christmas, people's gut flora takes such a pummelling.'

'You going to be back long?' asked Fionn.

She wavered her hand in the air, said, 'I just itch to be back over there. Everything feels political there. Even if it's not obviously so.'

'Any highlights, like?' said Fionn.

Arden, red-faced, dressed as an explorer from *Jurassic Park*, came into the room, excitedly clocking the air with their hands and crying: 'Snacks! Snacks!'

Close on their heels came Kostas, who uttered a wordless roaring.

'Kostas! Oh my God! Chill!' Milena cried, shaking her head, goggling at him.

Kostas merely giggled in response, and mounted the stubby kids' chair by the equally stubby kids' table, where his sister Eva was squirming around, ranking the gifts in her present haul to Freddi, who listened, nodding gravely.

'The Kuromi doll was the best one but the My Melody dress was a close second,' Eva explained, with newsreaderly gestures of her hands. 'Because I already have a My Melody doll, this was smaller. All I needed this year was to accessorise.' She swished a greasy bang from her eyes, then canted towards where Milena was lowering a plate of chickpeas and rice towards her.

Louise squinted at the big biffed head on Fionn and he gave her a palms-up shrug, trying for a nonchalance he did not feel: in fact, his skull was a balloon squeezed between two fists. He plucked at a button of his shirt but did not undo it, because then he'd draw comment for showing too much chest. What he'd give to be out in the park under the sleet, wind pummelling his head into thoughtlessness. He could drift around in the greenish shadows under the alders, their snaky branches, pretend he was in a horror film where nobody important died at the end.

To evade Louise's gaze he dandered, wobbly, with Brendan toward the food table. A heart chickpea masala and a dhal flanked a plate of vegan halloumi, the trio arrayed before a vast crockpot where bulgur wheat steamed. Thick flitches of rough-cut onion darkly caramelised were abob there amid chunked butternut squash. You could garnish this from two little minsters: one with tepid salsa verde, the other a far more attitudinal Carolina Reaper, under a sinister glister of oil. Even the basmati rice – seasoned with coriander and lime – was local: some Thomastown coffee roasters had expanded their line into an experimental paddy field, Milena had told them, with not unqualified success.

'It makes you less worried about the Apocalypse,' she said to them.

'Yeah, you know what, you do have to take the hope where you can, don't you,' said Louise, ladling.

While she and Milena exchanged loaded plates and bowls then passed them to guests Leilani moved among them with an armful of hot floury rolls wrapped in a white cloth napkin fringed in lilac.

'How'm I doing?' Brendan said to Fionn, as they filled their bowls.

'Oh, hardly noticeable,' said Fionn, as floppy tongues of aubergine slopped down. He could never tell how far gone he was going to get, or how much food would weigh him back into himself, but the little belly buzz kombucha gave you was kicking in, mellowing out the para feel. The room could be bigger, and looser, and cooler, but it was what it was. The floor-boards threw back too hard a shine for him to fully handle.

Willow had drawn closer to Fionn, stepping back out of Milena's way. Their shoulders were almost touching. She'd only on a string top, so he could feel the heat of her skin through his t-shirt. Willow was also hot, probably second only to Leilani in the room, to be fair, but in opposite terms: see-through pale, nearly, with a wavy tumble of black hair, and willowy limbs. A history of eating disorders had left her physique bulletproof against late-thirties spread – extremely hot, yes: but also mental, and therefore doubly, perhaps even triply so.

'Atitlán opened me right the fuck up,' Willow said. She shook her hair back, clamped it in her hands, then let it flow through her hands. Her body unkinked on the spot in time with the gesture. 'Anyone from a colonised country has the effects of history in their bones. Ireland, Guatemala, it's all the same – Gaza, obviously. So me being there was the marrow in me cracking and letting all that pain leak out.'

'Right,' said Fionn.

'I was there for Paddy's Day,' she said. 'Coincidence, you know. I hardly celebrate it. I say bring the snakes *back*, if anything.'

'And the witches,' said Fionn agreeably.

'And I just realised that we drink so much because we're traumatised up to our eyeballs, and that's the fastest way we know how to cope. But there are older methods. We have those in our bones, too. We're tree people. Poets. Wild things thirsty for God. I have believed for a long time that we bring something special to the world, just like all cultures do, and that we have one of the largest diasporas in the world because, once that thing awakens fully in Ireland, it will awaken across the globe. I don't know what it is but I can feel it. And sure, both Halloween and St Paddy's have been hijacked and commercialised as the biggest Irish exports after Guinness, but to be honest, I don't care; if it gets people noticing our weird little island floating off the edge of Europe, all the better.'

'Yeah,' said Fionn. The kiddos had installed themselves before the TV. On screen, the angsty hollering of a Latinx pre-teen merged into the sonorous roar of volcanoes bursting their tops all around.

'You don't sound convinced,' smiled Willow.

'Well, I don't know, it's just. Well. I have trouble with Ireland *having a moment*, or whatever,' he said. 'Feels smug. Or maybe just cringe. It's like too earnest.'

'But irony can be so toxic,' said Willow, probing.

'Ah, yeah, no, you're not wrong, like. Absolutely,' he said. 'But I just wonder about art being made from that place. It'd end up dull or. Maybe whiny? Or pandering. Like if you're just making an out-and-out creative vehicle for an argument or for empathy or healing or that it's just …' He was losing his thread. He squinted into his bottle. 'Artists aren't historically known for being good people, is what I'm saying, maybe.'

'No, yeah,' said Willow. 'But inferiority complexes and self-hate are *such* a colonial legacy.'

'Yeah, fair,' said Fionn, shifting his posture. 'But if you have a therapy-empathy thing driving art stuff then you wind up making it out like there's only two classes of people – the ones who suffer, and the ones who watch. And the ones who watch feel like by just watching and making stuff they're doing something when they're not.'

Willow smiled at him over the rim of her glass, but her eyes had a banked anger in them. Louise had drawn near.

'Does he turn everything into a debate?' Willow said to her.

'He can be stopped, sometimes,' said Louise.

Willow laughed, looked into her empty glass, and said, 'I'd better get some more before the kombucha's all hoovered up.'

'What was that all about?' Louise said to Fionn once she was out of earshot.

Fionn shrugged, said, 'We got into it a bit. About old Ireland, new Ireland.'

'Nothing that serious, then,' said Louise, and they watched Arden coaxing Kostas and Eva through a choreography based around the video on their phone. Though Eva was younger and chubbier, her movements were smoother than her brother's, and he sat down, arms folded, with a grunt of frustration.

Unheeded, the film about the Latinx kid and their journey of discovery continued. The child wandered dazed over a field strewn with flaming debris: shattered crystals, shards of multicoloured jewels and metal – emerald, lilac, jade, magenta. On some he can see the faces and hands of miniature gods. The world is so suffocating with tiny details, all of them laboured over, and he pays attention to so few of them. These immense, hysterical emotions are what he tried to get a grip on with that PhD idea of his. His particular interest was in the spectacle of mass death, those cities and housing units, those crowds, disappearing with bangs, cracks, booms, splats, crunches: sonic metonymies of destruction, ungraspable, head-to-foot oblivion, one human microcosm at a time. The point of plotted narrative, particularly in genre, was to take a political position, and then to make it seem universal and inarguable based on moral idealism as connected with visceral experiences of fear, pain, suffering and hope. The idealism and the politics underlying imperialist cinema's spectacles of mass death were grim indeed. But those pictures were even in kids' TV now. With a queasy, sidelong lurch of the stomach he asked himself if that was because part of the logic of fascist culture was to ensure that nobody ever grew up, and felt as impotent, as overwhelmed, and as red-facedly histrionic when big as they felt when small. Meanwhile, appeased, Kostas had been coaxed to his feet, and Arden offered their hand to him, which he shook with solemnity. He went back to the choreography with more enthusiasm but no greater precision.

'Were her arguments good?' said Louise, watching Willow talk to Freddi.

'You'd have destroyed her,' said Fionn, and Louise laughed. He loved her glassy brilliance. She deserved so much better than the university where she was teaching medical ethics but she was too spiky to get a better one. She couldn't pick her battles and wore out twice a term. He'd tagged along with her to one of her conferences once, to El Salvador. They'd scudded through a city that wasn't even that big, not by Latin American standards, anyway, with lights strobing across the windscreen. The rest of his memories were just of being a bit high in the hotel room while Louise sifted printouts on gender violence, looking for anecdotes that might prick and sting. He'd looked past a balcony rail stain-mapped with petrol fumes, gone on weed he'd paid too much for, a beer sweating in his grasp, saying, 'Wow, shit,' to the bits Louise quoted, a dizzy sureness coming over him that he'd seen nothing and understood less. From the combined smells of weed, fried food, and sea salt, mingled around the thud of Saturday-night clubs, Fionn had gotten a feeling of ambient promise, jeopardy, hope; a sense that a dozen or a hundred or a thousand nights out around him were taking off, at least some of which would end in exultant first-night sex, 5am coke-rails, multiple, newish, recondite forms of coupling. His night would not be among these.

'I feel like I've been invited to a catastrophe,' Louise had said from behind him at the table, her hands in her hair. 'But I'm only allowed look at it through perspex.'

From the balcony below a web of smoke went up thick as cotton gauze. On a walk alone earlier that day he'd overpaid for weed, bought from a dreadlocked guy in wraparound shades who'd had the torso of a footballer, then sprinkled it on a frozen pizza. She hadn't picked up on it because he'd said he was out of it because of the heat. But he was out of it because of the weed, a hundred per cent. It was tapping him into deeper truth frequencies than were permissible to admit, than were assimilable when brought back into the clear, weed-free thinking of later. Soon, it would be as if none of these thoughts had ever happened. Did that mean they had any truth value? If so, what was it?

He watched a thought spider and ladder hooking and unhooking eight unbreaking ink-blot knees, all finical, at once, and one at a time, somehow at the same time: all that free controlled motion. Louise's mind was like that, he'd thought to himself, and mingled with the prick of pride in her he'd felt envy seep out, too, bitter and warm, stronger than the love. Is this what they meant by *mixed feelings*? Was the experience of mixed feelings a sign of maturity as well as a cause of distress? Could it be both: an emulsion, a creamy beige of truth?

He was as stoned, as confused now in the Christmas room, with the others. Louise was looking at him, saying, 'Are you sure you're not out of it?'

'Oh, no,' he said. 'I'm just wondering if I want to find out what Willow thinks about trans people.' He had perhaps not said this quietly enough, because Louise squeezed his hand warningly.

She said, 'You only think you do,' but she was smiling as she said it. 'Let me go placate her,' she added, and winked, then was off to talk more to Willow, over by the pitcher of kombucha.

This left Fionn standing next to Tess. She was looking over with almost ferocious askance at Milena, who was going over a finer point with Leilani. It *was* weird, Fionn acknowledged, getting catering in. What were the ethics of making use of gig-economy labour like that? Probably suboptimal, he reflected, especially when it made the only other Black person in the room besides Tess a person who was paid to be there. Was that as fucked up as it looked or was it OK? Tess saw him looking and held up the ladle she was doling rice from.

'Seconds?' she said.

'Oh, no, I'm grand,' he said, and sidled over.

'How was your year?'

'On the shunty hurtle towards death,' Fionn beamed.

Tess looked at him, frowning, and let her glasses drop over her eyes.

'Did Brendan give you the happy box?' she said.

'He did, yes,' said Fionn.

'Then why're you talking like that?'

'I mean,' he said, 'I don't feel *un*happy. About the death-hurtle. Thanks, primarily, I'd say, to the box.'

'What the meditation teaches you,' Fionn heard Milena say, 'is that nothing actually moves in a straight line: it just looks that way because you expect to find that pattern in things. The trick is to unplug yourself from your naive faith in causality. Then you'll see how it was all just circular conjugations of the same material, ethereal and real.'

'I've always just held it down,' Tess said. 'And so, that's all I'll continue to do.' She pressed the heels of her hands to her eyes, pushing up her chunky-framed glasses so they tipped back, resting against the bunched minaret of her braids. The glasses were pale-orange Retrosuperfutures, chunky-big but with clean lines, like the maquettes that decorated her studio.

The shape of those glasses recalled the day he and Louise had delivered her the Puma bag.

Tess had received them, still in a neck brace, saying, 'You're allowed to say it's because I married a white guy.'

Behind her Fionn had seen the daybed she'd splayed out in the office for herself, a leopard-print thing with a Turkish kilim draped clashily over the bottom. Tess's grate was a proper old one. Fionn had gone in and raked cinders over the whitening dome of coals with an elegant metal wedge. Every little doodah there looked bespoke and cosy. Somewhere in there, maybe, just out of sight from the surface of her own mind, she'd been planning this move: and fair play to her, honestly; Jan was shite craic, if not actually a full-on abusive life-suck of a man. Tess texted furiously for a minute, then stopped, put the phone in her lap, lifted her hands to her temples. With eyes shut, she said, ‘Oh my God, I’m so sick of him.’

‘You need to start crushing your enemies, Tess,’ said Fionn.

She fixed him with a hard look and said, ‘My husband’s not my enemy.’

‘What’s he done now?’ said Louise, before Fionn could say anything.

‘He’s pissed I turned off location sharing,’ said Tess.

‘Why had you it on to begin with?’ said Fionn.

‘So he wouldn’t think I was having an affair,’ said Tess, and Fionn did not say, *But are you not?*

‘You can send him a photo of me as proof you’re not,’ he joked. ‘I can wield this.’ He’d lifted the elegant wedge. ‘Like this or more threatening?’

Tess looked back and forth between him and Louise. ‘It’s giving *intervention* having you both here at the same time, you know.’

‘I can leave,’ said Fionn, and Louise had said, ‘Yeah, maybe this is one for the girls, no?’

He’d gone to wait around the corner at a cafe then, tried not to let the bleed of resentment leak through him, because that would have been a Jan thing to do; instead, he had a flat white, read *Black against Empire* on his Kindle.

He had drifted off again, but Tess hadn’t noticed: she was texting, a frown on her face. He saw a chat icon with the word *JAN* and a familiar eggish noggin there.

‘I’ll leave you to it,’ he said.

‘Mm,’ said Tess in response.

Fionn eased himself down onto the couch. Between him and the TV, the kids were at the karaoke, using Arden's phone. Eva made an arc of her pudgy arm, palm up to the ceiling, and bellowed into the Bluetooth mic. Her grip on its stem wobbled, Dopplering the volume up and down. As her song ended she turned outwards, arm still in its arc, to take in the room. Kostas and Arden applauded. Eva surrendered the mic with a bow that flopped her hair forwards. Arden took the mic and offered it to Kostas, who refused with a headshake and a look of dread. Arden and Eva shrugged at one another, then sat either side of Fionn, while the film played on. Kostas, noticing he was alone, scrambled up beside them, his weight pressing the cushion down, making Fionn slide towards him. Kostas giggled at the contact, and Fionn patted him on the back, feeling a warmish bloom of regard fizz through him. He'd never wanted his own, but being around them was alright, wasn't it, the odd time.

Freddi was speaking German into his phone, head canted down, a finger in his ear, chuckling. In the corner, Milena was telling her other ex-flatmates how she and Freddi were just back from the Bamako Biennale, where – she relayed this in a lowered voice – they'd had a threesome with one of Freddi's co-panelists, a local. 'Milena!' hissed Tess, but even Fionn could hear the thrill of envy.

'We went on an app for the purpose: married hookups – discreet stuff, you know. And the first blip on the app we got, well, she'd been *showing us around* earlier that day. And four hundred metres away! And, well,' – she shrugged, looked not a little hungrily over at Freddi, who stood smiling down at the kids – 'that was that.' The instantaneity of Fionn's own jealousy shocked him, the sudden coring gouge of it, hot through his tripes.

'Like nobody'd say it was taking advantage,' Milena continued. 'She was older, not younger. An artist. And not emerging, but burgeoning. So it was all fine, consent-wise, even if you include the race and colour differentials, power- and privilege-wise. I think a moment of sexual egalitarianism, almost utopian, if I might be so bold.'

Fionn looked about him, at this generation that grew up learning about mores and expectations, but which had emerged into an adulthood when it seemed as though all of these could be ignored – although to what degree of flagrancy, that had never been clear to Fionn, meaning he'd remained neurotic well after the others, with even his permitted enjoyments and indulgences appearing furtive to him.

'It's not even that unusual to have a three-way,' said Louise, in a drifty sort of a voice, without looking at anyone. 'Not anymore at least. The statistics put it about the same as the percentage of cat owners.'

'Any plans for the Christmas?' he said to the kids.

'We're going to France,' announced Eva. 'For some winter heat.'

'Dad gets seasonal affective disorder,' said Kostas sagely.

'It's a hard old cross,' said Fionn, and Eva nodded.

'It interacts with his complex PTSD,' said Kostas. 'That's not like the one you get in wars. It's different. You can get it from parents and school as well.'

'I had no idea,' said Fionn.

'It can creep up on people, Mom says,' said Eva.

On the TV a girl in a white dress banded with colourful sashes scooted back, away from a cliff edge that reared prowlike into a suddenly opening void. Her plaits, worked into onion-shaped bunches, shook in a gust. Before her towered a goddess, hands on hips, laughing, her skirt adorned with medallions, her feather headdress immense and vivid emerald. In defence, the white-dressed girl raised her hands and hollered, shooting two great geysers of red lava towards the laughing godess. Fionn inhaled sharply and plucked his lip, cotton-mouthed and queasy.

'Who's these then?' he said.

'Purépechas,' said Eva absently, her eyes far, lifting a Hello Kitty soup spoon towards her lip.

Leilani drifted towards the couch, in the middle of a lull in her obligations, and stood by the arm of the chair, watching the TV.

'I didn't tell you,' Fionn said to her, in order not to hear any more of Milena's account, 'the last time. But I was there once. Brazil. In Rio.'

Leilani looked away from the screen, gave him a tight smile, said, 'Rio is so nice.'

'Couldn't get my head around the place,' he said, knowing he shouldn't keep going, but needing, all the same, to say something, so he wouldn't want to turn and see either the look of dissatisfied boredom on Louise's face or hear her say something about a curiosity he couldn't satisfy. 'Still can't to be honest. I was still in college like. But I started to think of life differently after. The violence in the place and the poverty and yet also all the lushness and the colour and the liveliness. And how happy the people are all the same. Or try to be anyway. Like in a politically defiant way almost you know. Not like here.' A memory came to him of a party, an at-ease perpetually grinning fella called Marcio whom they'd fallen in with, Marcio shucking the cork off a cava bottle with a show-off swing of his da's machete, a sudden pinkish spatter bursting across the garden's oxide-red clay, a sudden darkness on a redder darkness, one that faded almost instantly, guzzled by the earth. It had seemed to him then as an image of human life there, so replete and so profuse and thus so cheap, as though devalued by its sheer pullulating quantity.

'Yes, in Brazil it's often hard,' said Leilani, still smiling, sounding not a little wearied. 'So people just do the carpe diem thing I think.'

'It must feel very affirming,' said Fionn.

'Right,' said Leilani, eyes drifting, as though scanning for someone else in need of a sambo square. 'Is this why youse all seem so relaxed, being here? It's just less crazy? And it's like such a total relief?'

'I was relaxed in Brazil too. I think it's dispositional.'

Her smile tightened further. 'Another bread?'

'I should ask you for a playlist. See where you get it from. Hear where, rather.'

'There's some good Spotify ones.'

She held out a plate retrieved from the coffee table: vegan canapés, which he had not sampled. Fionn purloined for himself a pillowy breadslice topped with a bean paste tart enough to do for goat cheese, a pearly hazel, walnut's brainfurl, lovely warmy honeydrizzle.

'Tremendous,' he said, but Leilani had already gone on, pearly whites aimed at the next. *We haven't a clue*, he thought to himself. His childhood bloomed up through him: hubbed under the cowl of the blanket with his Beano Club torch, eyes flicking back and forth over pages so fast it nearly hurt, Atlantic 252 going – REM, Smashing Pumpkins, all the rest. What were Leilani's night sounds when she'd been small? Crickets, no doubt – and perhaps the buzz of overloaded wires, sirens' blue waul cutting the night? He'd seen that police series with the guy from *Narcos* in it, big rangy lads doing checkpoints, bag searches, pat-downs on schoolkids: and that was just the gang members. Stray bullets clinked and tinged ricocheting amid frying pans, a windowpane with the sodium-illuminated star of its own breakage there in the glass. Had she heard that? Had it happened at a friend's house? Worst he'd ever seen was Jamie Broderick's coffin toted down the nave, its wood the exact tint of chicken en croute, and the sick feeling turning over in his belly, thinking of road-safety adverts, all those red body bags laid out on an empty motorway's clean monochrome diagrams, that orangey red, the colour of the word *warn* in his head ever after. Walking out after the coffin he'd kept his eyes front so as not to see the lit-up coffin, the bulgy sunfish head and bloaty hands inside: the wax-encased bones of Saint Victoria Martyr, her head back on a puce satin cushion with tassels, her hair crowned with ceramic roses, eyes agape in numb ecstasy, and a tin chalice supposedly holding her blood. He didn't have to look to see her. He saw her in his head if he thought about her. She turned the liquid of his knees to glue and made his innards feel all shivery, as though the blood feeding them had turned to steam. She must still be in there, he thought, glooming up at the roof of her coffin. He felt ill. How could anyone want to go near any of that, honestly.

Fionn shut his eyes and eased his head back against the couch, letting the room become nothing only a soup of noise:

cork-pops, the tinkle of dropped caps, clinkings of crockery, sentences reduced to shreds and frays. For a time it didn't matter how boring he found himself, how few of the immense panoply of life options on offer from even this collapsing world he had availed of. He could forget his own existence and nothing would happen. He saw himself as a wooden mask topped with feathers, slowly disappearing under lilac sands that the wind chased endlessly across the desert. His atoms and the atoms of these imagined sands had begun to swap places, he was sure of it, this is why he felt himself fall and cease, away from pinpricks of white light, but then he felt something heavy land on his shoulders and he jerked up with a yelp, nearly clocking his skull off of Brendan's chin.

'*Bren-dan*,' said Arden, shaking their head. 'We're trying to watch.'

Eva munched on, untroubled.

'Sorry, love,' said Brendan. 'Just hazing the creature.'

'Where'd you go?' Fionn said to him, as he wiped the back of his hand across his mouth.

'I was feeling the whoosh of the earth through frigid interstellar space, man,' said Brendan, and pressed the heels of his hands against his cheekbones. 'Jaysus but 'tis strong.'

'No, I meant, like, where in the gaff did you go,' Fionn said.

'Oh,' said Brendan. 'Just lorrying into seconds. There was too many people for a bit. Now I'm alright. Are you alright?'

'Yeah, grand,' said Fionn, scratching his sideburn. 'Reckon if I've seconds I'll be comatose, though.'

'Some visuals on it though aren't there,' said Brendan, holding forth a napkin laden with flaked almonds.

Fionn took a pinch of the nuts and said, 'You're not wrong.'

Brendan shook and shimmied his shoulders and said, 'Wouldn't mind an aul' boogie all the same. This playlist is a bit of a downer, no?'

'It's Louise's conscious-rap list,' said Fionn. 'She does rowing machine to it.'

'Fair play, fair play,' said Brendan, scanning the room with a chilly voracity. Fionn could tell how impossible he'd have been when properly on the session back in the day. He felt grateful that the air was leaving their lives, deflating so slowly, so softly, away from a stress often mistaken for excitement. In the time he'd drifted off, Brendan had fallen in with Willow and Freddi. He got up to keep track of them.

'I give addiction treatments, yeah,' Willow was saying to Freddi. 'But with no judgement or labelling.'

'And would they be expensive like?' said Brendan.

'If money's getting in the way for people it's absolutely no issue,' she said. 'The point is they become the "you" they're meant to be.'

'That's sound,' said Brendan.

'I think thinking too much is the real plandemic of our time,' said Freddi.

'Overeducation is so real,' said Willow. 'Like, I'm not going to fetishise the noble-savage trope, but it is true that the less you have the more you give of that less.'

Brendan said nothing. He sucked on the happy box and nodded in time to the little scuds of vape he let escape his lips. He held out the happy box to Willow and she gave him smiling prayer hands before she took it.

'I haven't watched the news in months,' said Freddi. Now it was his turn on the happy box. 'I've never felt better.'

'You know there's a Media Addicts Anonymous?' said Willow. 'It's so real.'

'Yeah, I dunno,' said Brendan, arms folded, foot tapping. He shrugged. 'I just give money to fundraisers or whatever. Going places to see stuff just means people living there having to keep you safe and shit.'

'It's total main-character syndrome,' said Willow. 'The desire to bear witness. There are always people bearing witness at car crashes. They're called rubberneckers. Or bystanders. True witness is a compassionate seeing into the vulnerability of the other and reaching them there.'

'You're not wrong,' said Brendan, driftily, taking back the happy box. He stroked his throat and said, 'Need a wee drink if anyone wants one?'

Willow shook her head and Freddi said, 'No, thanks.' Fionn watched Brendan mosey towards the drinks table, then went back to sit on the couch again. There, he yawned and let his steepled fingers rest on his sternum, while the girl in the white dress with the onion-shaped braids battled lava demons with a sword of broken lightning.

At the same time, Willow's wood-heeled Chelsea boots clopped fast across the floor to the kitchen, a glazed look on her face. Her bowl deposited in the sink, she turned back the way she came, saying to the others, 'Must make an Irish exit now.'

'So soon?' said Louise. 'You've barely had a pick.'

'Date, though, haven't I,' she said, and touched a lock of hair back into true.

Louise said nothing. Fionn saw a confused emotion quiver the lines of her forehead.

'Double-booking,' said Milena. 'How gauche.'

'It's what Christmas is all about,' said Willow breezily, issuing kisses. 'You text your secondary-school crushes, you see what happens, and something happens.'

Although Fionn imagined it would be much lonelier in reality, he envied Willow's lightness. A sad freedom breathed off her as she headed for the door. He saw the bluish lights of a city stretch before her, saw the snug quiet of the taxi bearing her smoothly towards an assignation that, to him, had all the aura of a heist or a mission in an action film.

'You must let me run off now,' said Willow, giggling in Freddi's goodbye clinch.

'You don't want someone to bring you?'

'It's literally up the quay,' she said, gaily, manoeuvring from him.

Fionn turned back towards the loaded table with an uneasy twisting in his gut, looking past the food toward the squads of kombucha, kefir and ginger-infused non-alcoholic beers, arrayed triangular, like bowling pins. He never usually *needed* a drink, so much as just *really enjoyed* the one or the two of an evening, but in a moment like this one he knew what feeling people in films were meant to communicate when they flung themselves down on the bar as though beached up there by a wave and gasped out, 'A manhattan, stat!' or whatever. But there weren't even any desserts to glaum down, not really: you couldn't count fruit. His path of least resistance was perhaps the happy box but another bang of that would only make him spiral out altogether.

He was not the only one feeling this way: nearby, Kostas moaned for chocolate, or even just ice cream, and was negotiated with. An angry tearless sigh went up from him but he held out his palm all the same for the curves of satsuma his ma peeled into his grasp.

'There's so much sugar in fruit, even,' said Willow, who was belting shut her coat by the door.

'You're not wrong,' said Milena, as the peel uncoiled from her fingers in a long unbroken 'S'.

'Have a good one, Willow,' Fionn said.

She gave him a straight-line smile rendered knife-sharp by the absence of emotion in her eyes, then said, 'You know, when I took the medicine the first time, the shaman said to me, "There's nothing wrong inside you possessing you. You know what's wrong with you? You are."' She shrugged. 'I found it very healing.'

Fionn jerked his head back. Milena was nodding along to Kostas' ice-cream-centric petitions: she didn't seem to have heard anything.

Willow kissed her two fingers and lifted them to the room, then wiggled them, and said, 'Alright, that's me off,' and was gone out the kitchen door into the hall.

'But oranges taste like *air freshener*,' said Kostas, and stamped.

Fionn swirled his kombucha, watched the grains eddy and furl. If he stayed here on the couch he'd fall asleep – and, OK, so he knew everyone well enough to get away with it, but it wouldn't be quality sleep, and yet the lapse would probably mess up his solid seven, whatever time he got into it.

'You doing alright over here?' said Milena, approaching from the hall. She'd changed out of the party dress and into a comfier-looking striped Breton jersey with Mom jeans. It made Fionn feel relieved just looking at her. He pushed himself up from the couch.

'Ah, he's sound, really, Freddi, isn't he,' said Fionn, as Brendan nodded along, frowning with concentration, at Freddi's explanation of the metallurgical elements in his art.

'I'm not not a fan,' said Milena.

'How'd youse meet?' Fionn said to Milena, trying to distract her. 'Can't remember, if I ever knew.'

'On the apps,' she said tersely. 'A really dirty one actually.' She turned to Fionn with a setness to her jaw that he hadn't noted till now. 'Youse two it was in a bar, no?'

'You don't know this?' said Fionn.

'We've been together too long,' said Louise.

'Yeah, it's like youse have been together forever or whatever,' said Milena. 'Permanent.'

'We met on the apps of ancient times,' said Louise.

'A bar,' said Fionn, scratching his nose.

'Actually,' said Louise, her hand on his inner forearm, 'we first met *twice*. I was out with my friend and I'd been stood up. So we were just trying to salvage some kind of giddiness from the evening I guess maybe because we made a bet then that whoever got a number had to buy the other a drink.'

Fionn felt a spark and a flare behind his ribs, hearing it all again, seeing it all again: the garlicky taste of Mooseheads, the DVD box set of *Eastbound & Down* he'd bought to make himself less miserable once back home – and then, suddenly, Louise, with her magenta pixie cut and her badge-studded leather jacket, saying, 'I'm doing this for a dare, but you actually seem alright.' He looked at her retelling it to Milena and realised he was actually turned on: not just by the usual pattern-recognition that turned him on these days, which was more relief, on mapping the shape she'd been when he'd met her and the shape she was now and thinking how it wasn't as far apart as she worried it was. This relief, however, worried him, because it was more the lack of divergence than any in-itself attachment, as he saw it, and would this widening divergence lead to something worse in him?

'So I went over to where he was,' said Louise, with a warm grin at him.

'I was with my buddy, Derm,' Fionn issued forth chirpily. 'Whom some of you may know.'

'Yeah. And I couldn't see you from where I was, so I went over to go get the other guy's number. But there you were. I saw you. We talked. You were nice, I thought.'

'Then you left without getting my number,' Fionn said.

'I did,' said Louise.

'We had to meet again about nine months later in Dakota Bar before there was a number exchange,' said Fionn.

'That night was good,' said Louise. 'You were out with Derm again. And I was out with Tess.'

'A sterling wingwoman,' said Milena.

'She shifted Derm,' said Fionn.

'Derm is also a great wingman to be fair,' said Milena.

'Did they meet again?' said Louise to Fionn.

'I very much doubt it,' said Fionn, watching Tess take a puff on Brendan's happy box over by the sink. 'But it cleared the decks for us anyway.'

'Talked all night,' said Louise. 'Went for a kebab.'

'Top class,' said Milena.

'I'm a nervous man,' said Fionn. 'It felt daring to me.'

'Was there a first date-date?' Milena said, shifting posture, one foot out, a wine glass of kombucha resting against her underlip.

'Yeh, Yamamori,' said Louise.

'Haven't been back since,' said Fionn.

'Why jinx things?' said Louise.

Fionn directed the hose of the kitchen sink onto the forks and spoons, scouring off the toughest grease-lagging. Behind him a dessert-less dinner had led to some crabbiness among the kids, so Milena had Deliveroo'd up a cheesecake from an Italian place that was still open. The adults were now arrayed in a loose semicircle on yoga cushions around the telly, which had shifted on to a *Lemony Snicket* adaptation. He could hear Brendan mutter that the biscuit base was utterly class. Fionn pictured the Deliveroo guy who'd sped the cake to them through the thickening sleet, his bike treads grooving the slush into lines as neat as a vinyl record. Pure cold air stung his sinuses. He let buffet forth from his mouth a thick cloud of breath. Soon he'd be home with his family or his flatmates, the thermal shell no longer wobbling on his back. Something jolted upwards in his chest as he took in the ghostly shimmer of the trees in the fog. Teary eyed with weed and tiredness, Fionn forced a wettish, sentimental prayer from the meat of midchest, out to the lone imaginary cycling man as he flashed westward through bone-rattling cold past the Wellington Monument and its greyish nap of frost and meltwater, hoping he wasn't going back to a marquee of the kind he'd been arranging for this time last year.

'Maybe not brown enough for me,' Milena said. 'But oh well.'

Freddi squinted down the barrel of his kombucha bottle and said, 'Is this celery taste?'

'Celeriac,' said Louise.

Freddi squinted and said, 'Right.'

'I don't think I've eaten this healthily,' said Tess, 'since that retreat.'

'Oh my God are those the ten-day ones,' said Louise. 'Where you can't speak.'

'*And* get up at 4.20,' said Milena. 'It's only funny the first three times. Then it's funny again at the end. Because you haven't heard a joke in a week.'

'What did you do it for?' said Freddi.

Milena shrugged and said, 'I quite liked the quiet. Coming back was, like, super abrupt. All that noise and stress.'

'Your back was in bits for a good long time afterwards though,' said Brendan.

'They had me on a mattress on a reed mat,' said Milena. 'Which, to be fair, I thought would even me out. But it was just all the sitting. But then you're allowed talk if you've a complaint or some difficulty or whatever and when I said my back hurt from the sitting I was told these were impurities of the mind and to sit through them.' She pressed the knuckles of one fist into her lower back and corrected her posture with a grimace. 'God, I can still feel it.'

'She was on the standing desk then for a while after,' said Brendan. He looked over at Arden asleep on the couch. 'I sort of think we should hit the sack but I'm not inclined to move them.'

'Pick them up in the morning,' said Milena. 'They like Kostas.'

From the sink Fionn couldn't see the whole of Louise's face, only a certain rigidity to the profile, especially about the mouth. She brushed then plucked fluffs from her cords.

A loneliness in him reached out from his chest to a loneliness in her, a grotesque red stretchiness, fleshy and ending in a fist. Her head nodded a little to the playlist but he couldn't make out the song, even as he killed the jets of water from the hose. He wanted to hub himself around her, warm away the loneliness and distance in her, but he knew that would be an invasion, that he would cut her off from whatever revelation about her fundamental isolation that it was she was falling through, alone in herself.

'Dry that?' said Leilani, and he said, 'Oh, thank you,' and handed over the blue plate to her, but Louise had intercepted, and said, 'You go get a rest, Leilani, it's been a busy night.'

Leilani gave her bell-like chuckle and surrendered, saying, 'Well, OK.' She tried to do a last pass around the room with the fruit bowl but was urged to desist and get on home for God's sake. She received these instructions with another laugh and a shrug, then said, 'Well, alright. Happy holidays to you all.' To a chorus of thanks she began to don her russet beanie hat and a pair of mittens decked with snowmen. The snowmen bobbled as she waved and left the room to collect her coat. Milena, sitting back against the couch, arms out, let herself yawn, and Freddi said, 'This is perhaps as good a cue to dissolve the party as any, no?'

From the doorway as they were leaving Fionn could see the Liffey's dark line, the blue pallor of the street, a white-blue emptiness, and navy cirrus sucked flush to the curve of the sky.

'Oh my God, I can't wait to get home into the heat,' said Louise, stamping her feet, hugging herself. Fionn loomed around her in a hug. She stepped back into his embrace but didn't soften. He felt the bird-frail spininess of her. Her shapes prickled him inside, almost, seemed like, as though to pierce him, nearly.

'Let's get that door shut now and youse inside before the cold wakes the kids,' said Fionn.

'You're fine, you're fine, give us a hug for God's sake,' said Milena, reaching up to Fionn, who let go of Louise to give her a peck on the cheek.

'Was a class night,' he said. 'Thanks for having us.'

'Thank you best friend,' said Louise, her own arms spread wide.

'You're welcome best friend,' said Milena, beaming. Her eyes shone a little – tiredness, sentiment, both, who knew.

Fionn's phone buzzed: their Yaxi was here. Milena craned at the screen and said, 'Oh my God the surge pricing on that. Do you not want to hang on?'

'Bedfordshire is calling me,' said Louise.

'Brendan alright to sleep it off in there you reckon?' he said.

Milena batted a hand and said, 'I'm a past master. Long as Freddi doesn't seduce him or whatever.'

Fionn barked out an overeager laugh that made a frown quirk almost imperceptibly across her brow.

'Alright, homeward bound,' she said, with a last shoulder squeeze to Milena. 'Text you about that swim next week, yeah?'

'Hundred per *cent*,' said Milena, beginning to ease the door shut, as Fionn and Louise headed down the stairs. He threw his arm out around her.

'Really,' said Louise archly. 'You're very attentive.'

'Only to you,' said Fionn.

'Oh,' said Louise. 'I think you just love everyone.' She added a laugh that wasn't without good humour. 'But maybe only when you've been vaping.'

Fionn felt his body sag.

'It's not a big deal,' said Louise. 'It's Christmas. You're very nice on it, too.'

They mounted the Yaxi. Fionn said, 'Hiya,' to the driver, who bobbed his eyebrows at him in greeting. They peeled away from the kerb with a smooth whinous hum. Fionn eased himself back against the seat, head back, arm out, teasing his fingers through the hair that hung down Louise's cheeks. She smiled, nuzzled against him, eyes shut. He felt no contentment, not even any relief: only a slight dimming of the anxiety tinseling his ribs.

'That was alright, wasn't it?' said Fionn.

'I feel all bleak actually,' she said.

'You didn't even drink anything.'

'Maybe I should have put hooch in my kombucha.'

He loved the look of the sleet pattering the windscreen, which was a high one, a hood of glass that made him feel he was beneath the dome of a space pod. You only ever got a Christmas feeling these days, he thought, when a snowy one was at least notionally possible. Was that just maybe a nostalgia for when the right weather happened at the right time, or was there something deeper, more ancestral to it? That was Willow territory, though. He didn't want to go too far in that.

'What has you feeling bleak?' he said instead.

'Oh, I don't know,' said Louise, and Fionn felt a barb of worry sink into his mood. She always did this. 'Just. What even way out is there. We're all so stuck.'

'Stuck where, love?'

She shrugged in his hug and again he felt the boniness of her.

'Just,' she said, and blew out a breath that wobbled her lips. 'Oh, I don't know. Hearing about three-ways. And dates. And other people's setups or whatever. And then ours.'

Fionn said nothing. His chest tightened, frostily. In his head he saw again the imagined Deliveroo driver, felt that imagined cold as though it were his.

'Like I'm not saying I want to open things up or anything,' said Louise. 'I just. I wish there was a way to not feel so—'

'Clenched,' said Fionn.

'Inside,' said Louise. 'Yeah.'

They'd passed under a sodium light; its glow made her hair flame rich bronze.

'Like even if you run around you're still just on the thing you're running around on,' she said. 'There's no—'

Fionn felt his chest go up and down as a big breath came out of him, a slow, shingle-loaded wave.

'Transcendence.'

'Yeah. No upwards or outwards.'

'What was it Freud said,' he said to the top of her head. '"The only truly happy couple is a weed lad and his happy box?"'

Louise hmphed out a laugh through her nose.

'Thanks,' she said.

'For what?'

'For not being mad.'

'At what?'

'At me being weird and needing propping up all the time.'

'Sure we all need that,' he said. 'What was that song you were listening to inside in the gaff?'

'Which one? I wasn't keeping track.'

'When you were on the armchair,' he said. 'Staring into space.'

'Oh. I was doing that a long time.'

'You were nodding along to one.'

'I don't even remember.'

Light came down flatly on it all, making the sky's dome feel at once encroaching and far off, the slick underside of a blue polytunnel. Streaks and patches of slush retreated already from the slate roofs as they thawed. A burglar-alarm's red insectile light ticked on, off, on again outside the Four Courts. A shape slept under one arch, an orange sleeping bag, its tint somehow the colour of the word *warn* in Fionn's head.

Louise shut her eyes again. Slumped like this the lines of tension went from her face and she was twentyish again, the age she'd been when they'd met. He could call up enough memories to force the blood in him to quicken, to the point where he'd not only have sex with her before they slept, but also look forward to doing so, as much as in the days when she'd been newish, evasive, making every fuck seem like a scrabbling to grab her by the ankle, keep her, hold her fast beneath him. When he'd thrust on top of her, speeding to the end, heedless of her orgasm, because she'd had two or even three already and he could give way to his own, he'd find himself thinking the word *demolish*, without being sure what he was demolishing: her reservations, maybe, or the distance between him, or perhaps, worryingly, her freedom. But that couldn't have been true, because he hadn't felt like he was giving up any freedom by being with her. He'd felt freed from the panicked need to chase others, in fact. He'd hate to have any of that back. It wasn't as fun as it looked. It couldn't be.

'I couldn't imagine being without you to be honest,' he said. 'At this point.'

Louise sniffed in her sleep, smiled a little, stopped smiling, then said, 'Why, because we're nearing halfway so may as well stick it out?'

'Not like that,' he said. 'I didn't mean. I just.'

'I'm *teasing*.' She lowered her head to his chest. 'When's the last time, then?'

'The last time what?'

'The last time you imagined being without me?'

'Oh, ages ago,' said Fionn. 'Maybe the third date?'

She laughed, then said, '*That* long ago?'

'Well, it was just a weird energy,' said Fionn, flustered.

'Was it the cinema?' she said. '*Hot Tub Time Machine* wasn't it. I did find it offensive to be fair but that wasn't on you.'

'That was the second date,' he said. 'This was the comedy gig. The one where he kept saying I looked like all the Beatles stuck in a blender together.'

'That's right,' said Louise, pressing a palm to his chest for emphasis.

'I wasn't even thinking I didn't want to see you again,' he said. 'I was just thinking I was all off and nervous because of his nonsense and maybe you were thinking you'd had enough of being with someone this nervous so I was like mentally getting my attack in first or whatever.'

Louise said nothing for a second, then said, 'Honestly, I barely remembered it. We had sex that night, didn't we?'

'Yeah,' said Fionn.

'So then,' she said. 'Nothing to worry about.'

'It was just weird energy,' Fionn said, to flatten that one. 'Serrated. But that's the last time. It's smooth sailing since. For me anyway.'

'Mostly,' she said.

They were slowing along the canals. Willows hunched over the still black water. Two swans drifted, either still awake or awake already. Spume, foam, reed flinders, cans, and half-sunk burger shells floated a little way from them. He'd read a tweet that said they didn't actually mate for life, at least not monogamously; in fact they had one main partner but got up on whoever whenever – or was that swifts. Either way they were only birds, weren't they, although were people any better really all things considered. The car eased along the curve of the last street before home. Fionn followed the swans in the rearview mirror till they were gone, then flicked his eyes back through the windscreen, saw their door slow towards them. The handbrake gave a long slow ratcheting click. Fionn added 15 per cent to the fare and the app notification made the man driving them say, 'May it be multiplied coming back to you, sir.'

'Ah, listen, no, not at all, same to you,' said Fionn, flustered, embarrassed he hadn't added twenty or twenty-five, then got out, went around to open Louise's door for her. Sleepily, on wobbly feet, she smiled and got out, face ashen with sleep.

They were in and up fast to their apartment door then. It was near enough Herbert Park that they were paying too much for the size of it, but the location said it all, and there wouldn't be any kids, so it was fine, ish, at least insofar as anything was fine anywhere these days really when you thought of it, how impossible Dublin was, how even more so all the time. Louise leaned for a moment on Fionn's arm while she worked off her boots. A warm tenderness deepened in him almost towards lust. The intention was there for a shag. If none happened it wouldn't be his fault. He'd be respecting her tiredness. Fionn shot the lock to behind them. Together, coats off, they tottered down the corridor towards the big bathroom. He left her brushing her teeth then went and stripped down to his boxers. If he put on his lounge pants it wouldn't happen. He went back to her. His movement set off the sensor on the courtyard light: a spill of light fell through the frosted glass of the bathroom and over Louise's shoulders and drowsy face. She looked at him and blinked as she ran the electric toothbrush whining around her mouth, then spat.

'Sleepy,' she said, mushily.

'Yeah,' he said. 'Same, to be honest.'

She looked at him there in his jocks with no slippers on and said, 'Are you not cold?'

'Yeah, maybe a bit, actually.'

'Brush your chompers and go in and heat up the bed for me.' She waited for a pause in his brushing then kissed him with her toothpastey mouth.

He spat, rinsed, and went in to lie down. A stony abrasive weight was in his stomach. When she got in she rolled into the lee of his shoulder and he folded her to him. She gave him a kiss that had depth but no real welly to it.

'You never said,' he said. Here he was, auguring at the stony weight with another sentence he didn't want to say, in a voice he didn't recognise, it was that bland and smooth. But how else to make that feeling go.

'Never said what?' she said.

'The last time,' he said, 'you imagined us not together.'

'Oh.' A warmish sigh huffed against his skin. 'Ages ago.'

'But when, though?'

'Well, I was going to India, wasn't I?'

While a junior doctor – long before her academic pivot – she'd taken two months to volunteer at a children's cancer clinic in Kerala.

'But that was only for a summer,' Fionn said.

'Yeah, but I was giving it the *I don't want to hold you back thing*,' she said.

'All I thought was, *See you in two months*. Excuse to work on the PhD application, kill the time.'

He looked down and saw Louise smile, eyes shut. She wormed her forehead deeper into his armpit. Her weight on him hurt even though she was so light.

'I was trying to break up with you,' she said. 'But you just wouldn't get the message.'

'Well, clearly fucking not,' said Fionn, trying to keep his voice down.

'I loved that – *obduracy* in you,' she said. 'You knew what you had and you wouldn't be beaten.'

He felt the big wallowing stupid shape of his own body: a tall oval, even though he still thought of his face as belonging to a thin man. The fearful bafflement he saw there behind his glasses always surprised him. Why would anyone want to keep hold of that? He thought of himself as a chill guy, felt proud to be a chill guy: it was the relational-ethic ideal of his generation. You couldn't do anything about Gaza or structural oppression, which sharpened the imperative to not be a pain in the arse making things worse for other people towards actual urgency. He'd have been even worse when he was younger.

'What was it,' he said, 'there was someone else in India or—?'

'Oh, no,' she said, sleepy again, shaking her head. Her hair tickled his skin, itched it. He wanted to shunt her off, but that would be passive-aggressive – *aggressive*-aggressive, actually – so he didn't. 'I just—'

'Keeping the options open,' he said, and felt a cut feeling open itself inside: raw bared skin shining wet.

Louise shrugged. 'How often do you get to go to India?'

'But there weren't, in the end,' he said. 'There weren't any options.'

She shook her head, slowly this time, and smiled up at him, saying, 'Not a one.' But her voice was veiled and sad, which made the terror rise up through him again. He shifted around in a rustle of sheets, lay on his back with his hands behind his head, forearms on the cold bits of the pillow. They'd nearly split up and he hadn't even known it. He tried for analogies: a bus at the kerb, whipping past your nose, almost obliterating you; or when you felt tired swimming, knew that the sea's big muscling would go on whether you stopped in it or not. He'd been in a car that summer on a holiday with his buddy Aidan, a travel writer. They'd been driving from Novi Sad to Belgrade and the driver'd been nodding after too big of a lunch with one too many rakijas involved, and Fionn had thought to himself, *This could be it.* It would be a thing of nothing – a flip and an unfelt crunch he wouldn't hear, only feel in the big red cry of every tissue in him, but then that'd be it; a moment of confusion and panic and then nothing – the better-case scenario, within the circumstances, better for sure than coming round crippled under white hospital light, being told things about his condition in a language he didn't understand. He frowned at the fragility of it all. What if she hadn't walked in that bar the second time? What if she hadn't been stood up? These things had felt fate, but now he knew they'd hinged on a caprice, a decision not to break up that he hadn't been aware of – accident become his fate, and him there with not even a bluey's for fuck's sake. When had she changed her mind back? He shuffled up in the bed so that her skull wasn't pinching the skin of his arm. Why even ask? Why dig any more of the ground beneath his feet out from under him? He felt her twitch and soften, falling away from him into a depth of sleep he didn't want to trouble her out of, her breath coming and going in long tidal whisperings. A strange, friendly pity came over him. Sure she hadn't a clue what she was doing either did she. He put out a hand and ran his knuckles down her face from her temple to her chin, then butted the big one against the point of it, gently, before lifting a drool-wetted curl of hair from the corner of her mouth so it wouldn't tickle her awake. He lay down again, eyes shut, feeling a long slow falling that was bigger than his body, enough to shiver its outlines.

The bassy groan of a passing bus rumbled the apartment. A skizz and whoosh came then: a street cleaner, blasting away the refrozen slush. Sound was the sense of time, he decided, but couldn't develop the thought. Louise turned in her sleep and her head flopped, the softness of her cheek warm against the cool nub of his shoulder. They'd drift asleep like a pair of astronauts asleep in their pods while the house and the ground it was on revolved outwards into the immense swirl, same shape as they'd be if they decided on burial over cremation. Before the dinosaurs, bits of astral shit and dust had clotted together over billions of years, slowly coating a cooled chunk of magma. Then it had rained without end for a millennia or so. After that he was foggy: fish, somehow, then yokes on land, and now them, humans, who had a Neanderthal genocide on their conscience somewhere back there. Was that maybe the real ancestral guilt, and the Catholic biz was just overlaid? Could he have maybe cited that to Willow? She might have agreed with him then. He pulled the sheet up over him, past his shoulder, and yawned. A minute to midnight the weekend before Christmas, wasn't that what they said about humans, when they appeared in time if all of time was compressed into a single year. Must be about ten seconds left of it now and no new day guaranteed, still less all that probable. In how little time how spectacularly had they fucked it up. What were you going to do. Once again he was the wood mask he'd been, half asleep on the couch between the two kids. He saw the four planks that made him up darken in the water, saw the oily slickness coat the fibres from within, weighing him down. Slowly the planks fibred and began to drift. He'd no idea what the pictures meant. Maybe they were what it meant to know that one day none of any of anything anywhere anytime one day would matter and be as if none of any of anything anywhere anytime had ever been, whatever it even was anyway you know, or whatever the whatever and the it even were either, actually, come to think of it. Slowly the fibres of the wood mask drifted in tiny splinters, a widening spiral conjoining at last with the trash he'd seen afloat on the dark waveless canal around those sleepy swans cangled for good perhaps by nothing stronger than the plastic hexagon of a six-pack. Rain pattered down, a big hush, the colour of fog; his breath went out to meet that fog, a last upward flutter of the consciousness. He rested his chin on his wife's shoulder so his temple was snug to hers. Maybe this was as close as you could be to somebody: contiguity, not continuity. Maybe this was as close as you needed to be. Maybe this was all there was to any of it. Maybe a panic would come, ten years from now, feeling the last ignition of what little sap there was in him, and he'd get the yen for a fuck-frenzy that annihilated marriage, mortgage, career, all. Maybe he'd be on a drip at eighty and be unable to conjure up any memories of the life behind him but that of clattering away in the clamshell glow of one screen impatient to get home to the moonglow of another, bigger screen, this one with football on it. Maybe he wouldn't remember worrying about shit like this. Maybe he'd be too busy skimming his panic over every tissue and texture of his body, inside and outside, wondering which would be the one to give, at last, fatally, away beneath him. Or maybe he'd be too morphine-scattered to feel it as anything other than this sleep now climbing his limbs, a weight of black water, as still as the canals brimming in their lock-gates not even three streets over from them, awaiting release.

FROM *THE GREEN ROAD*

Anne Enright

published by Jonathan Cape

The next morning, she went early into Ennis. It was 10am on Christmas Eve and the supermarket was like the Apocalypse, people grabbing without looking, and things fallen in the aisles. But there was no good time to do this, you just had to get through it. Constance pushed her trolley to the vegetable section: celery, carrots, parsnips for Dessie, who liked them. Sausage and sage for the stuffing, an experimental bag of chestnuts, vacuum packed. Constance bought a case of Prosecco on special offer to wrap and leave on various doorsteps and threw in eight frozen pizzas in case the kids rolled up with friends. Frozen berries. Different ice cream. She got wine, sherry, whiskey, fresh nuts, salted nuts, crisps, bags and bags of apples, two mangoes, a melon, dark cherries for the fruit salad, root ginger, fresh mint, a wooden crate of satsumas, the fruit cold and promising sweet, each one with its own sprig of green, dark leaves. She got wrapping paper, red paper napkins, Sellotape, and – more out of habit, now the children were grown – packs and packs of batteries, triple A, double A, a few Cs. She took five squat candles in cream-coloured beeswax to fill the cracked hearth in the good room at Ardeevin, where no fire was lit this ten years past, and two long rolls of simple red baubles to fill the gaps on her mother's tree. She went back for more sausages because she had forgotten about breakfast. Tomatoes. Bacon. Eggs. She went back to the dairy section for more cheese. Back to the fruit aisle for seedless grapes. Back to the biscuit aisle for water biscuits. She searched high and low for string to keep the cloth on the pudding, stopped at the delicatessen counter for pesto, chicken liver pâté, tubs of olives. She got some ready-cooked drumsticks to keep people going. At every corner, she met a neighbour, an old friend, they rolled their eyes and threw Christmas greetings, and no one thought her rude for not stopping to converse. She smiled at a baby in the queue for the till.

'I know!' she said. 'Yes I know!' The baby considered her fully. The baby gave her a look that was complete.

'Yes!' she said again, and got the curl of a sweet, thoughtful smile.

All this kept Constance occupied until the time came to unload the contents of her trolley on to the conveyor. The baby held itself so proudly erect, the young mother underneath it looked like a prop. She looked like some kind of clapped-out baby stand.

'You're doing great,' Constance told her. 'You're doing a great job.'

The bill came to four hundred and ten euros, a new record. She thought she should keep the receipt for posterity. Dessie would be almost proud.

Constance pushed her trolley on to the walkway and the wheels locked cleverly on to the metal beneath them, and she was happy happy happy, as she sank towards the car park. She thanked God from the burning, rising depth of herself for this unexpected life – a man who loved her, two sons taller than their father, and a daughter who kissed her still when no one was there to see. She could not believe this was the way things had turned out.

Her feet were swollen already; she could feel them throb, hot in the wrong shoes. Constance bumped the trolley off the walkway, set her trotters thumping across the concrete of the car park. It was half past eleven on Christmas Eve. In the pocket of her coat, her phone started to ring and, by the telepathy of the timing, Constance knew it was her mother.

'What is it, darling,' she said, remembering, as she did so, that she had forgotten the Brussels sprouts.

'He's still asleep,' said Rosaleen. For a moment Constance thought she was talking about her father, a man who was not asleep, but dead.

'Well don't wake him,' she said.

Dan. Of course, she meant Dan, who was jet-lagged.

'Should I?'

'Or maybe do. Yeah. Get him straightened out.'

There was a pause from Rosaleen. *Straightened out*.

'You think?'

'Have you everything?' said Constance.

'I don't know,' said her mother.

'Don't worry.'

'It's a lot of work,' Rosaleen said, with a real despair in her voice; you would think she had just spent an hour in the insanity of the supermarket, not Constance.

'But I suppose it's worth it to have you all here.'

'I suppose.'

'I'll be sorry to see it go.' She was talking about the house again. Any time she felt needy, now, or lost or uncertain, she talked about the house.

'Right,' said Constance. 'Listen, Mammy.'

'*Mammy*,' said Rosaleen.

'Listen—'

'Oh, don't bother. I'll let you go.' And she was gone.

It was Rosaleen, of course, who wanted Brussels sprouts, no one else ate them. Constance stood for a moment, blank behind the crammed boot of the Lexus. You can't have Christmas without Brussels sprouts.

Sometimes even Rosaleen left them on her plate. Something to do with cruciferous vegetables, or nightshades, because even vegetables were poison to her when the wind was from the north-east.

'Oh what the hell,' said Constance. She slammed the boot shut and turned her sore feet back to the walkway and the horrors of the vegetable section. Then over to the spices to get nutmeg, which was the way Rosaleen liked her Brussels, with unsalted butter. And it was a good thing she went back up, because she had no cranberry sauce either – unbelievably – no brandy for the brandy butter, no honey to glaze the ham. It was as though she had thrown the whole shop in the trolley and bought nothing. She had no big foil for the turkey.

Constance grabbed some potato salad, coleslaw, smoked salmon, mayonnaise, more tomatoes, litre bottles of fizzy drinks for the kids, kitchen roll, cling film, extra toilet paper, extra bin bags. She didn't even look at the bill after another fifteen minutes in the queue behind some woman who had forgotten flowers – as she announced – and abandoned her groceries to get them, after which Constance did exactly the same thing, fetching two bouquets of strong pink lilies because they had no white left. She was on the road home before she remembered potatoes, thought about pulling over to the side of the road and digging some out of a field, imagined herself with her hands in the earth, scrabbling around for a few spuds.

Lifting her head to howl.

ABOUT THE AUTHORS

MAGGIE ARMSTRONG's debut, *Old Romantics*, was published by Tramp Press and Biblioasis. She has been shortlisted for Newcomer of the Year at the Irish Book Awards and for the Kate O'Brien Award. Her fiction, essays and journalism have appeared in *The Dublin Review*, *The Stinging Fly*, *Banshee*, *The Irish Times* and *Paper Visual Art*. She lives in Dublin.

NIALL BOURKE is originally from Kilkenny but now lives in London, where he teaches English. He writes both poetry and prose and, since completing an MA in Creative Writing at Goldsmiths University of London in 2015, has been published widely in magazines and journals in both the UK and Ireland. His poems and short stories have been listed for numerous awards, including twice for the Costa Short Story Award, the ALCS Tom-Gallon Trust Award, the Mairtín

Crawford Short Story Prize, the New Irish Writing Award, and the Fitzcarraldo Novel Prize.

In 2017 he was selected for *Poetry Ireland's* Introductions series. His debut poetry collection *Did You Put The Weasels Out?* was published in April 2018. *Line*, his debut novel, was published by Tramp Press in 2021. His second poetry collection – a 'choose your own poetry adventure' called *The Erection Specialists* – was published by Broken Sleep Books in 2022. He is represented by Brian Langan at Storyline Literary Agency.

SOULA EMMANUEL was born in Dublin to an Irish mother and a Greek father. She studied at universities in Ireland and Sweden, emerging with a master's in demography. She currently lives on Ireland's east coast. Her debut novel *Wild Geese* was published in 2023. In 2024, it won the Lambda Literary Award for Transgender Fiction, and the Gordon Bowker Volcano Prize at the UK Society of Authors Awards.

ANNE ENRIGHT has written eight novels, two books of short stories and a book of essays about motherhood. She was the inaugural Laureate for Irish Fiction (2015–2018) Her short stories have appeared in *The New Yorker* and essays, lectures and articles are published by *The London Review of Books*, *The New York Review of Books*, *The Dublin Review*, *The Guardian*, *The Irish Times* and *The New York Times*. She was editor of *The Granta Book of the Irish Short Story* (2011). Key awards include The Man Booker Prize (2007) – which brought her work to global attention – the Andrew Carnegie Medal for Excellence in Fiction (2012), the Irish Novel of the Year (2008 and 2016), The Writers' Prize for Fiction (2024), the Seamus Heaney Award for Arts and Letters (2025) and the Windham Campbell Prize. Her work has been translated into almost forty languages. She was born in Dublin in 1962, and stayed.

BRIANA FITZSIMONS is a mixed-race writer, educator and mother, driven to create the books she longed for as a child – stories that reflect the richness and complexity of the mixed-race identity. She holds an MSc in Creative Writing from the University of Edinburgh and spent thirteen years as a secondary-school teacher. Now lecturing at Dublin City University, Briana also delivers anti-racism training to educators across the country and is currently pursuing a PhD. Her award-winning debut, *Black & Irish: Legends, Trailblazers and Everyday Heroes* (2023), received critical acclaim and has become a core text in schools across Ireland. She lives in Co. Kildare with her husband and two children, and is proud to call Ireland home.

ARJA KAJERMO was born in Finland, grew up in Sweden, now resides in Dublin. She started drawing strip cartoons for the fortnightly magazine *In Dublin*. Her first book of cartoons *The Dirty Dublin Strip Cartoons* (Poolbeg Press) was a collection of *In Dublin* strips. She also wrote fiction and entered a short story for the Davy Byrnes Short Story Competition 2014. Her short story 'The Iron Age' was one of the six finalists. The novel by the same name *The Iron Age* was published by Tramp Press in 2017. The novel was longlisted for the Republic of Consciousness Prize and was one of the Walter Scott Prize's 'recommended reads'.

ROISIN KIBERD has written essays and features for *The New York Times*, *The Stinging Fly*, *The Dublin Review*, *Winter Papers*, *The White Review*, *The Guardian* and others. She is the non-fiction editor of *The Stinging Fly* and teaches Creative Writing at the University of Galway. Her first book, *The Disconnect: A Personal Journey Through the Internet* was published by Serpent's Tail in 2021.

MIKE McCORMACK comes from the west of Ireland and is the author of two collections of short stories *Getting it in the Head* and *Forensic Songs*, and four novels, *Crowe's Requiem*, *Notes from a Coma*, *Solar Bones* and *This Plague of Souls*. In 1996 he was awarded the Rooney Prize for Literature and *Getting it in the Head* was chosen as *a New York Times* Notable Book of the Year. In 2006 *Notes from a Coma* was shortlisted for the Irish Book of the Year Award. In 2016 *Solar Bones* was awarded the Goldsmiths Prize and the Bord Gáis Energy Irish Novel of the Year and Book of the Year; it was also longlisted for the 2017 Man Booker Prize. In 2018 it was awarded the International Dublin Literary Award. He is a member of Aosdána.

TIM MacGABHANN is the author of the novels *Call Him Mine* and *How to Be Nowhere*, the memoir *The Black Pool*, the short-story collection *Saints*, and the poetry collection *Found in a Context of Destruction*, which is out next year.

BELINDA McKEON is the author of *Solace* (Picador, 2011) and *Tender* (2015), and the editor of *A Kind of Compass: Stories on Distance* (Tramp Press, 2015). She directs the MA in Creative Writing at Maynooth University.

SUE RAINSFORD is an Irish novelist and art writer. She is a recipient of the VAI/DCC Art Writing Award, the Arts Council Literature Bursary Award, a MacDowell Fellowship, the Kate O'Brien Award and le Prix Imaginales Award. Her work has also been nominated for the Republic of Consciousness Award, the Desmond Elliott Prize, the Prix Jean Monnet des Jeunes Européens, the New York Radio Festival Awards, and the Desperate Literature Prize for Short Fiction. Notable commissions include RTÉ Radio 1 and BBC Radio 4, and she has been writer in residence at Maynooth University and UCD. She is the author of two novels, *Follow Me To Ground* and *Redder Days*, both of which have been translated into French.

JESSICA TRAYNOR is a poet and poetry editor at *Banshee*. Jessica's poetry collections include *Liffey Swim* (Dedalus Press, 2014), which was shortlisted for the Strong/Shine Award, and *The Quick* (Dedalus Press, 2018), which was an *Irish Times* Book of the Year. *Pit Lullabies* (Bloodaxe, 2022) was a Poetry Book Society Recommendation, an *Irish Times* Book of the Year, and a *Guardian* Best Summer Read of 2022. It was shortlisted for the Yeats Society Sligo / *Irish Independent* Poetry Prize. Essays and articles have appeared in *The Guardian*, *The Dial*, *The Stinging Fly*, *The Dublin Review*, *The Irish Times*, *Paper Visual Art*, *Tolka*, *Winter Papers*, RTÉ's *Arena*, and RTÉ / New Island's *Sunday Miscellany 50*. In 2019, she co-edited *Correspondences: An Anthology to Call for an End to Direct Provision* in support of MASI with the actor Stephen Rea. She is a 2025 EU Press Prize Laureate, was the 2024 recipient of the Tundish Award from Field Day for contributions to the arts in Ireland, and the 2023 recipient of the Lawrence

O'Shaughnessy Award for Irish Poetry. Her fourth poetry collection, *New Arcana*, was published by Bloodaxe Books in September 2025.

SOPHIE WHITE is a novelist, essayist and podcaster from Dublin. She holds a First Class Honours degree in Sculpture from NCAD. Her first four books, *Recipes for a Nervous Breakdown* (Gill, 2016), *Filter This* (Hachette, 2019), *Unfiltered* (Hachette, 2020) and *The Snag List* (Hachette, 2022) have been bestsellers and award nominees. Her fifth book, the bestselling memoir *Corpsing* (Tramp Press, 2021), was shortlisted for an Irish Book Award and the Michel Déon Prize for non-fiction. Her sixth, *Where I End* (Tramp Press, 2022) was described as 'brilliantly visceral' by the *Guardian* and 'exquisite and disturbing, brutish and beautifully crafted' by the *Irish Times*. It won the Shirley Jackson Award for best novel. Her fifth novel, *My Hot Friend* (Hachette, 2023) won the An Post Irish book Award for Popular Fiction. Her latest book, *Such a Good Couple* has just landed in shops. Sophie writes a weekly column 'Nobody Tells You' for the *Sunday Independent LIFE* magazine and her journalism has been nominated for numerous media awards. A TV adaptation of her first book is in development and she co-hosts the chart-topping comedy podcasts, *Stop The Madness* and *The Creep Dive*.